Otto A. De La Camp

A Spiritual Tour of the World

In Search of the Line of Life's Evolution

Otto A. De La Camp

A Spiritual Tour of the World
In Search of the Line of Life's Evolution

ISBN/EAN: 9783337194390

Printed in Europe, USA, Canada, Australia, Japan

Cover: Foto ©Andreas Hilbeck / pixelio.de

More available books at **www.hansebooks.com**

A SPIRITUAL TOUR

OF THE

WORLD

IN SEARCH OF THE LINE OF LIFE'S EVOLUTION

BY

OTTO A. DE LA CAMP

"Whatever is truly beautiful
The same is beautifully true"

BOSTON
ARENA PUBLISHING COMPANY
COPLEY SQUARE

PREFACE.

THIS book comes into the world in a manner somewhat resembling that of all children: it felt attracted, and here it is, anxious to be recognized and welcomed by all whose sympathies it can excite.

It is designed to appeal to those who are interested in studies concerning the spiritual motive of our Universe and the nature of our destiny.

Though this book may not bring any knowledge that has heretofore been foreign to the minds of men, it endeavors to unite some of that which is already ours into a picture both truthful and pleasing to the eye of the soul.

The sign of Truth being *Simplicity*, the author has made it his special object to evolve this "mind-picture" of the Universal Life by the very simplest means within his reach, so that it may reflect itself with clearness as a well-founded and well-connected thought-form into the mind of him who reads. Succeeding in the accomplishment of this object the author hopes that this little work will not be refused its modest part in the promotion of our spiritual enlightenment and well-being.

Sincerely,

THE AUTHOR.

February, 1896.

CONTENTS.

CHAPTER.   PAGE.

      PREFACE, - - - - - - - - - iii

      INTRODUCTION, - - - - - - - - vii

  I. THE WORLD'S FUNDAMENTAL PRINCIPLES:
     SPACE, SUBSTANCE, AND MOTION, - - 1

  II. TIME, - - - - - - - - - 11

 III. DIVERSIFICATION OF THE ELEMENTS; THE
     WORLD'S SYSTEM, - - - - - 18

  IV. ESTABLISHMENT OF ORGANIZED LIFE, - - 25

   V. NATURE OF THE PRIMITIVE ORGANISMS; CON-
     DITION OF THE EARTH'S SURFACE AT THE
     TIME OF THEIR FIRST APPEARANCE, - - 32

  VI. PLANT-LIFE, - - - - - - - 40

 VII. DEVELOPMENT OF THE ANIMAL BODY, - - 46

VIII. LIFE OF THE ANIMAL SOUL, - - - - 54

  IX. FORMATION AND NATURE OF THE HUMAN
     BODY, - - - - - - - - 68

   X. CONSTITUTION OF THE HUMAN SOUL; ORI-
     GIN OF THE RACES, - - - - - 77

  XI. UNFOLDMENT OF THE HUMAN SOUL IN THE
     LIFE OF THE COMMUNITY, - - - - 85

 XII. FATE, WITH REGARD TO PLANT AND ANIMAL, 96

CHAPTER.   PAGE.

XIII. VARIETY OF FATES AND CHARACTERS ON
THE HUMAN PLANE, · · · · · 104

XIV. THE REASON FOR OUR SUFFERINGS; OUR
RELATION TO THE EVIL, · · · · 117

XV. LEADING TO AN EXPLANATION OF THE INE-
QUALITY OF OUR FATES, · · · · 133

XVI. THE SOUL'S IMMORTALITY AND NECESSITY
FOR RE-APPEARANCE ON EARTH, · · · 143

XVII. CONDITIONS GOVERNING RE-APPEARANCE;
EVOLUTION BEYOND THE HUMAN PLANE, · 154

XVIII. CONCERNING THE HIGHER FORM OF LIFE
AND THE WAY IN WHICH IT IS ATTAINED, 162

XIX. OUR RELATION TO THE WORLD OF THE
DISEMBODIED AND TO ONE ANOTHER, · 180

CLOSING REMARKS, · · · · · · 202

INTRODUCTION.

You will agree with me, Kind Reader, when I say that our well-being, both individually and collectively, is largely dependent upon our conceptions of the world in which we live.

We, like all other creatures, being destined to seek and to find our salvation through our own efforts, thus naturally have an interest in the manner in which these conceptions are evolved : we are anxious that the comfort which they are to give be not merely temporary, but lasting ; and to this end, they must, of course, be children of the Truth.

Where is the Truth ? It is to be found everywhere within the reach of him whose eye can see it. We approach it by the simultaneous motion of body and soul: while the body with its senses moves around, taking note of exterior qualities, or the appearance of things, the soul proceeds to travel through, for contact with their inner nature, their reality; and neither of them permits the other a final rest. Each point reached by the senses of the body attracts the soul, the ceaseless questioner, with the result that our contemplated period of rest unexpectedly gives place to an interrogation; and this must, by its nature, urge us forever onward. Thus we continue everlasting wanderers through the Universe, consciously or unconsciously searching for a glimpse of Truth.

The experience, the knowledge, which we acquire on our way, will be gratifying to us in accordance with the nature of our observation. We, who desire above all things to behold life and well-being, can, of course, feel firmly established in a condition of serene contentment only when our experiences have generated within us the conception that this desired life and happiness is the ultimate fate of all beings. When this conception becomes inseparable from our inner life, we shall feel that our travels and attention have not been in vain.

Now, we perceive that this World may be searched for its Truth with reference both to its personality, and the motive which causes it. The personality, we find, shows us the perishable, and that alone; for it consists in nothing else. Therefore this cannot be the final object of our study. If we would know what lives beyond the personal, we must, of course, search beyond the same for that which has moved it to come forth and causes it again to disappear; we must study the motive power. How? By rising out of the personal into the Universal and identifying ourselves with the Universal character. There alone is to be found the motive which we are in search of; and in proportion as we succeed in imbuing our senses with this character will they be able to see that which controls our life and happiness.

As our studies always consist in individual effort, we can never lose the benefit which they bring us. We know that a view of the World from the personal standpoint, being our first proceeding, is pleasurable so long as we have not yet fully awakened to the sense of the perishable nature which belongs to the affairs of this life. When we have arrived at the perfect understanding of their true character, then we begin to feel the necessity of rising into the higher knowledge. This proceeding we find, however, attended with rather more difficulty, more painful effort, than the former. But, in all justice, the reward is in proportion greater; for it brings us the true conceptions which alone can permanently satisfy.

Therefore, we make this greater effort; and when it can be done in company, it will be so much the more enjoyable to each. You are

aware, Kind Reader, that this is my intention at
the present moment; and if it is likewise your
good fortune and desire, for the time being, to
enjoy a short freedom from the world of personal
cares and pleasures, I would propose that we
attempt such a spiritual tour of the World in
company. I promise that the same shall be as
agreeable as I can make it, and that no feeling of
disappointment shall come to you other than such
as may arise from the discovery that the regions
traversed are already familiar to your mind. This,
you will admit, could not be helped; for, may one
find anywhere in this World a view which some
eye has not seen before? But we find pleasure
in returning even to familiar earthly scenes so
long as they accord with our taste. If this is
true with regard to the material, how much more
must it apply to the spiritual! Let us then in
good faith proceed: —

CHAPTER I.

THE WORLD'S FUNDAMENTAL PRINCIPLES:
SPACE, SUBSTANCE, AND MOTION.

As we have already observed, the tour which we are to undertake is twofold: while our personality moves around the objects, the soul is to penetrate their surface and view them from within. We desire to discover the motive of life, the heart of the Universe; and the only way in which this may be done, is by observing how the Universe unfolds its life out of the first principles, and how it then proceeds in the course of its further evolution. Having, to this end, left behind us the sphere of our own personality, we are duly prepared for entrance into this greater one, the Universal, which comprises them all.

Let us, then, make our first move: We will proceed to a point somewhere in close proximity to our own planet, the Earth. What is now the first to attract our attention? It cannot be our person, the one in the midst of the many; nor can it be any beauty of surroundings. The first now to appear to us must be that which is most simple, most generally represented; it must be a fundamental feature of the World. So, in looking about, upon the Earth, its waters, and the surrounding heavens, we perceive, before all else, the bare existence of *Space*, *Substance*, and *Motion*. To the eye of the person this is, of course, a rather dry observation to begin with, but not so to us in our present attitude. The World's secret that we are searching must necessarily be anchored at the World's foundation; and therefore these three principles are the first objects to attract our attention.

We observe that they make their appearance simultaneously, and the reason for this is that each of them would be non-existent without the other two. A space implies motion: a point must move to form a length; the motion of this length creates the width; this, in turn, proceeds to form the third dimension, height. Also is implied in a space the coexistence of a substance; for, in order to be perceptible, a space must either be filled or be surrounded by the same; otherwise it can in no sense even have existence. Substance requires its volume of space as generated by aforesaid motion. And, lastly, we see that Motion cannot be without the necessary space and the moving object, distinguishable from its surroundings. Here, again, is required the presence of Substance, however fine this may be, and though it be no more than the substance of mere thought. Thus, wherever we look, we find these three principles simultaneously present, an harmonious trio at the World's foundation.

Let us now look into their interior and see them in their inner nature, their reality. Here we encounter the first unavoidable test of our independent soul-power. The nature of the Universe, like that of music, is comprehensible by way only of our own inner power of perception. The personal sense perceives the arrangement; the meaning is discernible only to the higher sense, the impersonal, the universal. That which we perceive at the foundation applies, of course, to the whole structure; and, therefore, whatever we may learn respecting the nature of Space, Substance, and Motion is really a necessary part of our knowledge if we would properly expand our views of the world of life which is evolved from these three principles.

We will, then, go nearer to the Earth and pick for our investigation some smaller object: here, this cocoanut; — what is its size, the space which it occupies? We compare the same with something smaller, for instance, its kernel. Then we look in the opposite direction for something larger. Thus we determine its relative, or apparent size. Now we want to measure its absolute extent as it is to be discerned from the universal point of view. To this end, we must find the smallest unit and also the limits of the whole of which it is a part. The inch and foot measurement cannot help us here. We retire once more into the interior of our cocoanut, towards its center. Here we begin looking for the smallest point, the unit. We magnify our power of vision. We find, that what at first seemed the very center-point, now proves to be a little sphere surrounding a center, which, before, we had not noticed. We look still more sharply and discover within this second a third. We see that we might continue thus forever, magnifying our power and discovering new center-points, each containing within itself one that is still smaller. We cannot find the particle which is next in size to nothing, and must conclude that it lies in the realm of the Infinite. Now we will come out of our cocoanut and proceed once more in the other direction : no sphere is so large that it may not be surrounded by one still larger. The limits of the whole must likewise be in the Infinite.

Where is this Infinite which contains the universal measurement of Space? From our personal point of view it is certainly beyond our reach. We will search for it through the universal eye. Our first view showed us the ever-present harmony between Space, Substance, and Motion. For instance, the form of a cube is wanted: In order to effect its creation, necessity calls for a point, a line, and a plane, specifying certain limits and directions of motion, — a demand which is always perfectly defined in all respects. It is responded to. The cube is now to be made in a certain proportion larger: point, line, and plane come forth and form it. We see, that, wherever a demand of necessity is thus clearly defined, there is a power present which fulfills it. Certainly, this power must be equally as definite in character, or it would not create with such precision. Looking about us, we find that it never fails, and thus we must acknowledge that there cannot possibly be any other power in existence. It is the undisputed regulator at the World's foundation, and, in accordance with its character, there must come forth from it a definite World. Whatever is to be cannot come into being in any other way than by the will of this one power, which we thus recognize as the supreme Law.

Supposing a form of indefinite proportions were wanted: could it come into existence? Law, which is always definite in its perception and power of execution, can, of course, respond to such demands only as it clearly perceives. Now, here we have one which is not defined and not clearly perceptible. The Law finds nothing to which it may conform its will, and leaves this form uncreated to remain in the sphere of the impossible. Thus we observe how the undefined is hindered from existence by the world of the definite so long as the character of the former remains undecided.

This very nature we have discovered to be the attribute of the Infinite itself. Therefore we may know that this Infinite does certainly not exist as a reality in this Universe. But may it not surround the same? We must conclude that this would always require the existence of Space; and wherever we find its attribute, extent, there we also find Law, which is ever the same, and which gives to this space, according to its nature, definite form. Go where we will, — everywhere and forever exists the definite. The Infinite is not there, and no eternal process of any kind can bring it forth: it is fatherless; and the ever present Law, not recognizing it even in the idea, can give it no form. So the Infinite can never trouble us. But it also leaves us without our desired discovery of the smallest and the largest sphere ; and thus we unexpectedly become aware of the truth that there is no actual measurement for Space, no Law of actual size : *Space, in the absolute, is sizeless.*

However, we may know that an actual size is not needed. Why not ? Because the absence of necessity is proven by the absence of Law. Let us demonstrate this : If actual size is not needed, it must be possible, for instance, that our whole solar system, in all the relative proportions of its parts, be made manifest within the space occupied by this nut. Can Law establish these manifold proportions within so small a sphere ? Yes : and we may also continue reducing, and at the same time adding as many more solar systems as we wish, forever, without reaching that smallness of point which they are capable of occupying in their exact relative dimensions. No sphere is so small, and at the same time none so great, in which Law cannot maintain them just as we see them existing around us ; for, whatever part of Space may be chosen,— so long as that part is a space, it will always admit of an infinite number and variety of divisions.

Supposing we, together with all existing proportions, were demonstrated within a sphere so near in its extent to nothing as to form but an idea of space, — would anything reveal itself as wanting in its present, well-adjusted size? Again, supposing all proportions were established on the largest scale conceivable, — could we perceive a difference? By no means. Thus we find that Law is in all its demonstrations independent of a specified absolute extent. No being can ever have cognizance of an actual dimension, and therefore none experiences the want of any. It lies not in the logic of Law to bring forth what is not demanded by necessity; and, there being no such call upon Law in this case, Space does not assume in any of its parts the character of actually limited extent. This means that it remains undefined in every part, infinite throughout; and therefore we know that it is barred from actual existence. The sole reality represented in it is: demonstration of relationships between parts. Thus we find Space to be merely an *idea*; it expresses the Law of *relative* proportions, and nothing else. We find it here, there, everywhere; for a well-defined idea, demonstrative in any dimension, must fill out with its being all existence. And yet, it lives not in locality; for there is none but the imaginary which is embraced in this idea.

What do we gain by this discovery? Let us apply its truth in our study of this cocoanut: The size of the nut, as we have now seen, is an ideal one; the space which it occupies is merely a demonstration of proportion to other dimensions. What, now, is its substance? This, we know, cannot exist outside of this imaginary and only Space. An ideal Space can contain no actual Substance. We must, therefore, conclude that this nut, as well as everything else which has the character of Substance, is as ideal as the Space which it occupies, — that there is not an atom of actually rigid Substance in the Universe: As we recognize in Space the demonstration of the Law of relationships between ideal dimensions, so we find Substance to be the demonstration of the Law governing their proportionate impenetrability, or density.

Now we throw the nut away and observe how it moves through Space. As we see it go, we feel assured that there is no power which can ever take this bit of substance from the Universe; for, without its Space, motion is impossible. But, at the same time, considering the nature of this Space, we see that Motion, like Substance, constitutes in the absolute but an *idea*. Being the third in this fundamental trio, it represents the Law which regulates the changes of position between the other two.

Thus we have succeeded in obtaining a view of all three principles as they appear in the universal sense, and therewith we have discovered the nature of all that is evolved from them.   We now recognize the Universe in its true character as being the great idea of ideas, filling out all existence by virtue of this trio of harmonious principles.   And in that which maintains this ever present harmony at the World's foundation we have sensed the presence of a Universal Spirit.

CHAPTER II.

WHILE our eye thus views the world of demonstrations as concentrated into the one ideal and omnipresent point called "here," we become cognizant also of another essential: the uninterrupted existence of the "now." Is this likewise an extent, or, as it were, another feature of Space? Let us examine it: As we have seen, the dimension known as length owes its being to the spiritual motion of a point. However quick this motion may be, we know that it takes place, or there would not come forth the idea of lineal extent. The World is thus filled with straight and curved motions. But we perceive also another variety: the degrees of velocity. And this is the one which suggests to us the idea of the feature called "*Time*."

We measure Time as we measure Space, that is, we take note of its relative extent. And, as a space appears large or small, according to the

closeness of attention bestowed upon the same;
so an extent of time will seem to us long or short:
long, when our power of perception is directed
away from the events to the line of their succession; short, when our interest is confined to the
events themselves. The marking of Time by
comparing the motion of the pendulum with those
of the minute- and hour-hand is our measurement
of relative duration. The absolute must be
sought by way of comparing the shortest interval
with the longest. We will first look for the
shortest, the unit of Time. This we know to be
that part which is marked by the shortest event,
the quickest vibration. So we proceed from
those executed by the pendulum to measure those
of sound. We find the much quicker vibrations
of heat, light, electricity. Finally we are led to
conceive of those originated by thought. These
latter are, of course, the quickest of which we can
have any knowledge. Now, the realm of thought
extends through the whole World as direct spiritual vibration, and we can understand that the
finer and more intricate a thought, the faster must
be the vibrations living in the same. But we also
conceive of the truth that no thought can possibly
be so fine, so elevated, so active, as not to admit
of one that is still more so: the quickest vibration

is impossible to be found, and will ever remain in the realm of the Infinite.

We now proceed in the other direction. Here we follow the slower vibrations, the revolutions of the heavenly bodies; the Earth, the Sun, the clusters of Suns, and so on, beyond conception: the longest interval is likewise an impossibility. Finding no limit in either direction, we are thus convinced that Time is really but a feature of Space, a fourth dimension, and consequently of the like ideal nature. We may see in it the demonstration of the Law which governs the relations between the various degrees of velocity of motion.

We assured ourselves before, that the other three dimensions of Space have no actual, that is, rigid existence, by demonstrating the absence of necessity. Now we must be able to proceed in like manner with regard to the fourth feature, Time. Let us see: If a specified or actual extent of Time is not needed, it must be possible for all the proportions existing between the intervals of which it consists, to manifest themselves unaltered within any space of time that may be specified. For instance, the events of an hour must be contractible in their right proportion to each other into the space of what we now call a second. This is possible, and their duration as a

whole may be reduced still more.   In fact, there
is no moment so short that it may not contain
them in the same relationship to one another as
we perceive them to be in at present ; for, as we
have seen before, there is no moment so small
that it cannot be divided into an infinite number
of others.   At the same time, the amount of
events thus contracted might be increased to that
of a day, a year, and so on, — infinitely.   "But
we are not to become aware of the fact that a
change has taken place."   How could we, since
our lives themselves remain confined in the midst
of the line contracted?   As it would be impossible for us to discover any deviation from actual
size, if such existed ; so would it be beyond our
power to perceive any contraction or expansion of
an actual Time.

Thus, the appearance of a space of time depends solely upon our own attitude towards the
same ; a moment, in reality ever so short, may
yet seem almost an eternity, and vice versa.
Time being thus elastic in appearance, no matter
what actual length might be assigned to it, —
why, then, should Law institute a rigid moment?
There is no call for one.   The necessary *must*
exist, the unnecessary is fatherless.   Therefore,
since the succession of events is merely a dem-

onstration of relative duration, without any distinguishable actual extent, we see, that, in the Spirit, all the past and all the future are so infinitely concentrated into one point, as to be actually contemporaneous. Our personality can, of course, never comprehend aught but succession of events, durations that are apparently real ; but in the Spirit, Time is all one moment, an inevitable and consequently *indestructible* ONCE, in which is contained simultaneously everything that is possible of existence through the power of Law. Can we imagine that any one of the Spirit's dictates has ever not existed and not been instantly fulfilled? We see, for instance, that when a combination is formed of certain values, or numbers, the total value, or end result, has its existence simultaneous with that formation. It is our person only which has to go through the process of tracing the relationships between these numbers from one stage to the other before the existence of the ultimate becomes apparent to us. And there is never more than one result possible ; for the Spirit's character, its Law, is ever clearly defined throughout, and therefore admits of no choice. On looking about, we find that there is no exceptional event anywhere, none which can not be traced from cause to cause as being the necessary and only possible result of the Spirit's dictates.

Thus we become aware, that, as the events of all times are contained within the Spirit simultaneously with its own existence, and consequently also with one another, each of them must necessarily be visible at any time to the eye of the impersonal observer. Is this manner of observation a possibility to individual senses? We must acknowledge that it is; for we know that a person's desire and powers of perception may at times be lifted entirely out of the ordinary sphere of the personality. Being thus hindered from acting in their own interest, they will thereby not be confined in idleness, but will be forced to operate in the world of personalities surrounding. There being to the senses thus liberated neither an actual distance between objects, nor an actual interval between events, all past, present, and future things of any locality will become discernible with equal clearness; and the senses will take note of all that towards which they are directed, perceiving in accordance with their individual ability and character. The fine thread of personal consciousness by which their connection with the body is maintained, is just sufficient for enabling them to impart their discoveries to the descriptive faculties of the person, and through this to the outer world. These are the essentials to the mysterious process known to us as clairvoyance, clairaudience, — constituting the gift of prophecy. And the more we contemplate the fact that individual powers of perception do occasionally in this manner reach beyond the sphere of the personality, discovering with equal facility things near and distant, past and future, the more strongly shall we feel impressed with the truth that our World is purely spiritual, ideal. Likewise does the conviction grow upon us, that our Universe is not brought into existence and maintained through the united action of various ideas, or Spirits, coming from independent sources, but that all is the perpetual unfoldment of one uniform idea, one character, well-defined in every particular, perfect, and therefore ever present, — One Almighty Spirit.

CHAPTER III.

DIVERSIFICATION OF THE ELEMENTS; THE WORLD'S SYSTEM.

In the light of the knowledge which we have thus far obtained we are now qualified for proceeding to observe our World more with regard to particulars.

We have already found, while contemplating the character which lives in the three fundamental principles, Space, Substance, and Motion, that there never can have been a time when this World did not exist, and, likewise, that there can never come a time when it might be destroyed. For, character means will, preference of one thing to another. The Spirit, being so perfectly defined in all directions as to comprise all Time as its own idea, always was and always will be as it is. Its character prefers to demonstrate itself, to continually unfold all the possibilities of its being; therefore we may know that Spirit and World are ever one and simultaneous.

Now we look upon all the many things which constitute its life. What a variety is manifested in the moving Substance, from the most ethereal to the most impenetrable! And what variety of motion and velocity!— not a point anywhere which is not being traversed by some kind of matter in motion straight or curved, slow or fast. Surely, these three principles are inseparable under all conditions.

All vibration, we find, is but the inner motion of the substance through which it passes; moreover, the various kinds of matter, or rather Spirit-substance, must themselves be so many different modes of inner motion, or they could not be so susceptive to all the vibrations coming to them, and yet retain their individual characters throughout. We know, that, for instance, the vibrations which we recognize as heat are produced through friction of particles. These latter must be impelled to violent motion before the heat comes forth and informs us of the vibrations which are taking place. But does this imply that there is no inner motion when the substance is in a state which we call "low temperature"? The fact that we do not perceive a vibration does not prove that there is none present. If one degree of warmth is produced through inner motion of the substance, all other degrees must arise from the same cause. And where is the line between heat and cold? It is only we who make such a distinction; in the absolute there is none. There we find the scale of temperature uninterrupted by any dividing-point; and thus we find that there really are degrees of one kind only, — degrees of vibration. And which is the lowest degree; which the highest? There is no limit in either direction; and, as everything that exists must possess a certain temperature, we become aware that there is not a particle of substance which is not in a constant state of inner motion of its own, however slow this vibration may be, — it is nevertheless present.

We observe that these vibrations differ, not in respect to degree of velocity alone, but also with regard to their form as determined by the nature and condition of the vibrating substance. We find this fact illustrated, for instance, in a body of water: The inner motion of water may be regarded as being ordinarily of a kind somewhat circular; for we notice that the particles have great facility for flowing, or rolling over one another. When their temperature becomes very low, so that crystallizations appear, we may know that their vibrations have not only become less active, but have also changed their form; for the particles have ceased their flowing motion and now cohere more firmly in the form of ice. In the opposite direction, the speed of their vibrations may be increased until the friction between the particles becomes so powerful as to cause them to disperse in the form of steam. The vibrations of iron, for instance, must be different from those of water; for their response to foreign vibrative power is not the same. This difference is perceptible even to our sense of touch; the sensation produced by hot iron is very unlike that which is caused by water of the same temperature: the feeling which we experience on touching the iron is more acute; therefore the vibrations of iron cannot be so smoothly round as are those of water. Thus, each kind of substance has its individual mode of inner motion by which it is distinguished from all the other kinds, in respect to both form and impenetrability; and we may here even go so far as to conclude that the indestructibility of substance is really nothing else than the exterior evidence of the immortality of the spiritual vibrative power within.

We have thus acquired an idea of the manner in which the Spirit diversifies its substance and effects change of condition. We now observe the great centers of vibrative power, the Suns, which radiate their force in all directions, penetrating with their life the things surrounding ; and, from the planets to the smallest particles of ether, we find all motion, all life.

An extensive view of this universal motion tells us that it is not a promiscuous motion, but that all is embraced in one great system which is brought forth through the principle of mutual attraction between parts.   Each attracts the others according to its character and power, and the greatest, the Suns, form the common centers ; these, in turn, cluster around another ; this, again, moves around a third ; and so we might continue forever finding new centers of attraction.   It is all a demonstration of close relationship between parts.   That this power of attraction is ever present and almighty, is certain ; for, if substances were not impelled to exert themselves towards forming this general union, their continued motion would soon disperse them and thus dissolve the Universe.

What causes this tendency of the parts to unite ? It can only be the affinity existing between their inner motions, their natures, proving them all to be of the same source and pervaded with the same Spirit.   They are forced in a certain sense to perceive one another's presence, whether they be mere minute particles or great heavenly bodies ;

and their effort at uniting shows that there exists between them a certain understanding, a degree of harmony.

We find, however, that a permanent union between individual parts is nowhere permitted. Not a particle of water, for instance, may remain forever in its ocean. It must sometime come to the surface; here its tiny spiral revolutions are joined by the kindred ones of the atmosphere, which bid it "come;" the ocean would have it stay, but the drop is already aroused to quicker motion, greater power, than that possessed by its fellows underneath; and the same law through which it is enabled to exercise its character in individual motion, now bids it assert the same, — to rise out and "move." The Law gives it a separate mission. And who can follow, even in idea, the wanderings of this drop of water through all the foreign elements, until it is permitted to return into its own, — for a while! So has the same Law, through instituting difference in degrees of power, given individuality, motion, separation, to the heavenly spheres. The Sun also says to the Earth, "come," and the Earth would fain unite, but the Law again says, "move." The Earth, too, has received its mission, and must wander until it is fulfilled.

What is this mission ?   We are aware that the Spirit does not stop in the unfoldment of its ideas with the demonstration of mere fundamental principles ; we see that it moves in them for further evolution, and that thus the World of heavenly bodies serves as its personality, or medium only, through which this object is to be accomplished. We perceive the Spirit's aim to be the demonstration of Existence, Motion, Life ; and a glance over the surface of our Earth acquaints us with the unmistakable evidence that this is the great mission of the planet : *the Evolution of Life.*

CHAPTER IV.

ESTABLISHMENT OF ORGANIZED LIFE.

LET us now give our full attention to this sphere of many combinations of which our personality is one. What a variety and abundance of living beings do we find around us! — all children of the same Earth, formed of its substance and sustained by it. How did all this life originate?

We know that the Earth could not evolve a single creature without the help of the rays of light and warmth coming from the Sun. We become aware that in these we are to recognize the bearers of the life. But now the question occurs to us, " Why should life demand the existence of the planets, when it already exists without them?" We may find an answer: We know that a Law exists only where it acts, — where there is an object for its demonstration. For example, the Law which directs that twice two be four, exists only where this number of things is present. Where could it be without them? This, of course, is only a very simple feature; but we know that the character of the Spirit remains ever the same, pervading its smallest and its greatest features alike. The nature of one determines that of all: if one of them is dependent for its life upon demonstration, the others are likewise. Thus we see the great reason for the existence of this Universe: the Spirit does not feel its existence otherwise than through the demonstration of its life in a personality. We, who are both of the Spirit and of its personality, may infer from this that the part of life which we represent in the Spirit would likewise be unconscious of itself, apparently nonexistent, if it were not projected into a body of some kind of vibrating substance. Thus can the life which radiates from the Sun become apparent to itself and the World only where it enters the substance and conditions necessary for the demonstration of its character. In the light of this observation we are now cognizant of the spiritual cause of both Sun and planets.

To explain the original, the innermost nature of this life, is, of course, impossible. It remains hidden to the personal senses, because it is of the Spirit; and it cannot be defined by the spiritual, by reason of its being so axiomatic that an explanation is altogether unnecessary. We know that only the necessary can exist; therefore we may conclude that such an explanation will remain an impossibility forever. Life is as self-evident as the fact that a moving point forms a line. This also is inexplicable; but, this truth being so simple, the mere knowledge of the same is sufficient. Now, each of the Spirit's possibilities is such a point, a well-defined idea; it continues, it moves, and the inexplicable, because self-evident, line of life is there. As the Spirit is present and in motion within all its particles of substance, so does it also direct the combinations which it forms of these. In every point it says, "I am." These demonstrations of relationship or contrast, as we know, constitute its life; and when we consider also what constitutes its character, we shall see why its next step must be to appear in the various forms of living creatures.

We understand that the Spirit's character, from its very foundation, is that of oneness, harmony. This attribute we have discovered while viewing the foundation of its World. And yet we perceive that all its combinations of mere matter are constantly dissolving one another, forming new ones, and that none remains by individual effort intact. Thus we see that matter alone can form no nucleus for further evolution. But evolution is the Spirit's object. Why? Because it is the only means by which relationship and contrast are brought forth. Now, evolution is possible through the medium only of superior harmony, *organization*. Thus we observe, that, in order to create a greater variety of contrast, more life, the Spirit reflects into the World more of its character of oneness. It establishes among its various combinations of substances harmonies that are more powerful, more enduring, than the rest, by means of organizing these harmonies and giving them individual being, so that each may remain clearly defined and distinct from all the others. The superior force through which it thus unites substance into organisms is, as we are already aware, evolved in the Sun, the centralization of vibrative power. Each ray, as it goes out from the Sun, is possessed of the higher form and degree of vibration which has been evolved from the union of all: it is thus the representative of a superior harmony. Reaching the Earth, the effect of these rays must be in accordance. Their vibrations are now, by virtue of their superior adaptability, enabled to enter the manifold combinations of inner motions which constitute the substance of the Earth. Harmonizing with each such combination separately, and steadily continuing their action upon it, these vibrations succeed in giving rise within the same to that superior harmony of motion which we know as individual *feeling*, or *soul*. Thus we see how superior harmony of vibration in substance forms a new kind of relationship, a further growth of existence through the establishment of greater contrast.

Through organization of these various modes of vibration into one harmonious power their tendency to maintain themselves against foreign influences has become concentrated into one which has the strength of all combined. There is thus present, not only the greater power, but also the stronger desire, which arises from the evolution of mere vibrative force into feeling; and, thereby, the maintenance of the organism in the midst of the world of unorganized matter is doubly insured. The creature is enabled, not alone to resist the World surrounding it, but also to absorb from the same such substances as are required for continuance as an individual being. The same life-vibrations, which, through the heat which they produce, cause the constant emanation of the creature's substance, also give the creature the power to replenish the same, and more, — we see that the being *reproduces* itself. But how comes this? Does it absorb more life-vibrations than it can hold, and, so to speak, overflow with

life? This must certainly be the case. We
know that the vibrations of substance without life,
although they may change in effect, yet never
cease. Therefore we may infer that those which
bear the life must certainly be likewise imperish-
able. Now, as these enter the being in profusion,
it is plain that they must give way to one
another; and so, eventually, they influence the
creature to form, of its own substance, bodies of a
nature similar to its own. In these young bodies
they then issue forth as new organisms.

Why does the Spirit institute this process?
Would not the same nucleus, once established,
suffice for all further evolution? We must consider the nature of its combination: We see that
the inner motion of the creature, its power of
feeling, is kept in constant exercise through all
the influences which are being brought to bear
upon the creature. Each experience leaves its
imprint. Each facilitates the reception of the
one following. Now, we are aware that the combination of substance and life-vibration which constitutes the creature clearly defines its character
and consequent manner of perception. This
means that the creature is limited to one certain
variety of experiences. What lies beyond the
being's power of identification cannot act upon its

powers of perception and feeling with the result of developing these beyond their limited sphere of consciousness. Thus, being restricted to receiving always the same kind of experiences, in the same manner, with the same consequent impression, the creature's inner motion gradually becomes so familiarized with them, that, finally, a further impression upon its feeling, or consciousness, is rendered impossible. The power of inner motion becomes indifferent through continued sameness of demands upon it. The creature at last ceases to perceive and to respond to them; it has perfectly absorbed all the kinds of experiences which were possible of attainment through this body, and therefore finds cause no longer for maintaining it as an organism. Thus we see that further evolution is dependent upon reorganization, reproduction of body.

CHAPTER V.

NATURE OF THE PRIMITIVE ORGANISMS; CONDITION
OF THE EARTH'S SURFACE AT TIME OF
THEIR FIRST APPEARANCE.

WE will now, in Spirit, move round about among these various lives and observe how they unfold. Where shall we begin ? With the smallest, simplest being, of course. But how is this to be found ? To be sure, not through the eye of the personality. We may magnify our power of vision as everlastingly as though we wanted to discover the smallest point, — and the earliest form of life does not appear. One ray of sunshine and a point of matter is all it represents. We must once more look through the eye of the Spirit : Is there a highest thought ? No : there is always one still higher, and it takes a creature to think it. Therefore, the scale of life is, in this direction, without limit. Could we find a limit in the other ? We find the scale of values in general to be without end. Whichever value we establish as the starting point from which to count degrees, — we shall always find the same to be exactly in the center of the scale. Degrees of life are values, also, and therefore we need not further look for the lowest nor the highest. The various lives, like all the other demonstrations of the Spirit, represent the idea merely of relative degrees, contrasts amongst one another. As we shall find ourselves, wherever we may go, always in the center of Space, so, no matter how high we may rise, shall we yet be in the center of the scale of life; and thus we shall never be able to discern either end. We may, however, feel assured beyond a doubt that each being, great or small, comes to the World with a mission to fulfill, which is as well defined as the creature itself. There has been a call of necessity for each, or it could not come.

Now, as we are not able to identify the smallest, simplest being, we will content ourselves with surveying the general characteristics of the class to which it must belong: The lowest form of life must certainly be that of mere vegetation. Wherever the life-vibrations coming from the Sun meet with the required conditions, there must result a corresponding creature, a nucleus for further development. The life of those which mark the primitive stages of existence must be simple indeed. These beings cannot be capable of anything beyond striving to adhere to the environment in which they first appeared, absorbing from the same whatever harmonizes with their nature, and meantime giving birth to other bodies of their kind ; then their own dissolves again as quietly and quickly as it came. These primitive beings must have already existed upon the Earth long before the elements had parted sufficiently to form a solid surface such as we see at present. While the solar vibrations, which are never lost, helped in the gradual separation of the light substance from the heavy, the thin from the dense, they must at the same time have given rise within this chaos of substance to a great variety of life.

It is, of course, not in our power to form within our mind an exact picture of the condition in which our planet was when the first signs of life made their appearance here. Nor can we at the present time obtain any reliable information concerning the first stages of unfoldment through which the various creatures passed, and which have eventually led to the great variety of species as they now appear around us. But we may rest assured that at some remote time each species was represented by creatures of the most primitive resources only, and that each species was then compelled to evolve the faculties which characterize the same, slowly and through the individual effort of the beings representing it. For the Spirit expresses in its creatures the Law that all powers are to be evolved solely through the medium of experience and exercise. The first stages in the evolution of planetary life may be surmised in their general outline only. We will make an attempt:

We may imagine the Earth to have been, by reason of its greater heat at the time, without a solid crust. Instead, it was enveloped by a number of strata differing from one another with regard to density of substance, the most attenuated stratum forming the outermost sphere. The creatures which came forth in this region received the strongest life-vibrations and the least substance, — were therefore the most active. Then, in their order, came those below : the greater the density of the strata in which they came forth, the more substance was theirs, and the less life. All these beings now floated about aimlessly, without finding any permanent hold; for there was none. Each, however, remained in or near the stratum to which it originally belonged by its character and density ; and, as each in turn transmitted to its offspring, not only its own general nature, but also some of the powers evolved during its individual existence, the species as a whole were thus naturally enabled to keep pace with the changing conditions of their environment. So, when finally a solid surface formed, those which had remained at the bottom, had already rendered themselves equal to the occasion by having evolved the various kinds of roots which this new condition required of them. Their life-vibrations being of the weaker kind, these creatures were more dependent upon a lasting hold; and so, in following their tendency to take root in the spot, each according to the nature of its substance and environment, they gradually developed into the various species known as *plants*. As the dense vapor hovering over this newly formed surface became more and more clarified, and, at the same time, the ground assumed its irregular altitudes, some plants became exposed to the influence of air and consequent stronger life-vibrations, while the remainder continued below, under the water. Thus resulted the variety of land- and water-plants, differing in degree of unfoldment and delicacy, but, originally, of the like nature. We may, indeed, find many of the species in the water represented correspondingly on the land above.

As we just observed, all life was at first mere vegetation. The organisms moving about in the currents of their different strata had no consciousness of any outer motion; they were completely at the mercy of all the influences that came to their environments. In the lower strata there was more tranquillity by reason of their greater density. The creatures living there partook of this nature and, as we have seen, fastened themselves permanently to the soil. Those in the higher regions, however, were subjected to influences more disquieting; they were moved about with greater violence. At the same time, they themselves had been more favored with rays of life-vibration, were comparatively less substantial, in fact, of an entirely different combination, and possessed more activity of their own. Thus, while those below were settling down to a life of tranquillity, these creatures were, in the course of generations, compelled, from both without and within, to adapt themselves to an existence altogether different. Of course they, too, were bent upon attracting to themselves and adhering to whatever came within their reach and could serve their purpose. That part of their surface which was the most receptive performed the work of absorption, while the parts surrounding this "mouth" became more and more employed in the work of adhering to that which was to be fed upon. Now, while being tossed about in violent currents, the creatures continually collided with all kinds of matter, and their powers of adhesion received the corresponding exercise, which had to be both sudden and energetic. That which seemed agreeable was drawn and held ; the opposite was, with equal energy, thrust off. During this exercise alternating between opposite directions the parts employed, of course, gradually, from generation to generation, grew in power, developed into individual character and form, and eventually hardened into the various muscular limbs. With their development also grew their demands for gratification ; and so, when the elements were finally separated from one another as we see them now, — into land, water, and air, —there was to be found in each a variety, not alone of plant life, but also of beings which had evolved the power of self-directed motion from place to place. Among these, as among the former, the plants, we find certain strong resemblances between species of one element and those of another, proving that, originally, their natures were similar. Although the same Spirit dwells in all creatures, whether they live in the air, the

water, or upon dry soil, the latter kind are
favored with the best conditions for the unfoldment of that which is in them.   We will therefore
direct our chief attention to the evolution of life
upon land, beginning, of course, with observing
the attainments made possible on the lowest
plane, that of plant-life.

CHAPTER VI.

PLANT-LIFE.

As we have seen, the plant is the organism which is favored with the lowest degree of activity. Its life-vibrations are comparatively slow and weak; but they are, on the other hand, proportionately sure and persistent. In its concern for the preservation of self in the midst of a world of change and motion, it fastens more and more securely to such favorable spot as it has happened to drift into. Here it now adapts itself as best it can to all the good and bad influences of its locality. In compensation for this, the plant then finds itself in position to obtain all its requirements without further effort than that of reaching out below and above ground and assimilating the nourishment, air, and sunshine thus gathered in. Having once succeeded in establishing its hold, it is now free to spread itself as far as its power of growth will permit. All the rest of its attention is left to direct itself towards the maintenance of its character, first in the individual self and then, through reproduction, in the species to which the plant belongs.

Now, as we are aware, the different combinations of substance must, from the very start, form a variety of plants, the characters of which likewise differ.   Also do the various climates exert their powerful influence towards diversifying character. These two particulars, therefore, cause and govern the great variety of vegetation which covers the Earth.   Wind, water, animals, and man, — all have then done their part towards the distribution of the seed, and have thus caused its growth to become promiscuous.   Look into a garden and behold what manifold expressions of plant-life may exist and thrive in close proximity to one another: Here is a huge pine-tree; close by we find a slender grape-vine.   How these two differ in nature and appearance!   While the pine uses almost all the nourishment which it absorbs, for the purpose of strengthening and enlarging its roots, trunk, and branches, bearing needles for leaves, and hard, dry cones for fruit; the grape-vine, on the contrary, develops so much root and stem only as is required for passing its nourish-ment through, forming great leaves on the way and gathering the greater part of its substance at the ends in the form of juicy berries.   Then see

the contrast between these two and yonder carrot,
which is almost all root. Again, compare the
huge stem and blossom of the sun-flower with the
cabbage-plant, which is nearly all leaves. Then
contrast, for instance, the tulip with the violet :
the one, holding high its gaudy blossom of weak
odor ; the other, hiding in modest seclusion, yet
filling the air with delightful perfume. Indeed,
on closer observation it appears to us as though
every characteristic trait that we can conceive of
were symbolized in some species of plant, — as
though the vegetable plane were, so to speak, the
unconscious reflector of the animal and human
characters. Each plant, from the clinging para-
site to the sturdy, independent oak, from the
offensive carrion-flower to the beautiful, health-
giving rose, suggests to us some particular trait
to be found actively demonstrated on the planes
above.

To be sure, all these manifestations of distinct
and permanent characteristics in plant-life are not
maintained by what we call deliberate, conscious,
individual preference ; we see that they are originally determined by the nature of the substances
and life-vibrations to which the plants owe their
existence. Each plant then maintains its individual character simply because it cannot have any

other; its own is the only one which it can ever know as being in existence. For, the same roots which help the plant to its tranquil life of self-indulgence, also hinder it from coming into conscious contact with the various other characters with which it is surrounded. Each plant remains in the midst of its associates an isolated being, limited in the exercise of its soul to the simplicity and sameness of experiences which characterize its life. Thus, a rose-bush, no matter how highly cultivated, will always remain but a rose-bush, a senseless plant and helpless sufferer of all the influences which may be brought to bear upon it. And the only means by which it can give voice to its inner life, are its vibrations of odor, — emanations of its own substance, which, however beautiful they may be, are still the most primitive of individual life-manifestations. Thus we see that on this line of evolution the organism is not designed for any higher attainment than that of developing into beauty and perfection as a *plant*. On this plane the Spirit establishes character and feeling as rudimentary ideas only. We find plant-life to be but a foretokening of that which is to come; it is a preliminary manifestation, though nevertheless an important link in the great chain of evolution.

Observe how the manner in which the organism endeavors to gratify its desire for self-preservation at the same time decides the limit of its unfoldment. The same tendency which leads the creatures to fasten themselves permanently to foreign substance, eventually hinders them from rising out into a higher sphere of life.

We see, then, that life may be further evolved only through improving its manner of preservation; and this improvement must, in the present instance, consist in introducing into the creature's life the idea of letting go its hold and moving from the spot. Forced, involuntary motion will not do : it must be self-directed.

This power of independent motion requires that the creatures possessing the same be more conscious of existence than the plant; they must be favored with a higher form of life, and consequently also with a superior kind of body. Their general nature has already become apparent to us during our study of the conditions which first caused them to take form. There we saw that these creatures, the *animals*, indeed originate from a superior kind of germs; that they have, from the very beginning, been favored with a greater share of life-vibrations as well as with a body constituting a superior combination of substance.   The animals, being thus altogether of a higher nature, constitute a plane of life clearly distinguishable from that of plant-life, — a higher plane.   At the same time, however, we perceive that the various species of animals differ among one another, like those of the plants, not alone as to inner activity, or life-vibration, but just as much in respect to the original combination of the substances from which they came forth.   This fact is evidenced alone by the difference in the character of nourishment required by the various species.   We will, then, continue our tour and enter the kingdom of the animals.

CHAPTER VII.

DEVELOPMENT OF THE ANIMAL BODY.

GREAT are the possibilities contained within the idea of independent motion. Increased motion truly means increased life. Let us, then, give our first attention to the evolution which this higher mode of life effects in the body of the creature. We may take for granted that animal-life, like that of the plants, was represented from the very start by a great number and variety of specimens at the same time; for the Earth, being round, and performing revolutions of a regular character, was enabled by the help of the Sun to offer favorable conditions simultaneously in the whole circumference of various latitudes. Now, in their primitive stages of evolution, as we have already observed, these beings can have had in operation no other force which distinguished them from the plant, than the mere power of motion. We are aware that they had also a greater power of inner motion; but their animal-faculties were still all in the germ, awaiting their development in accordance with the Law, which says, "Growth through Exercise."

These creatures now moved about promiscuously, bent upon obtaining the wherewith to preserve their lives. Their waste of tissue being greater than that of the plant, and their bodies being thus designed to feed upon other life, they were compelled, from the start, to aggressiveness toward the outer world; each preying upon the other, each, in turn, was forced to fight for the preservation of its own existence. It is only natural, that, in the course of such repeated demands upon the animal's sudden and energetic activity, every power of which the animal was capable gradually, in the course of generations, evolved into full growth, each faculty establishing and developing for its permanent use a special organ. So, from at first sensing the other beings upon contact merely, that is, feeling and tasting them, the animal soon began to perceive them at a little distance, through the vibrations of odor. Then it developed the faculty for receiving knowledge coming from sources more remote, in the form of sound; and, finally, it placed itself in conscious correspondence with the delicate vibrations of light. The comparative degree of development attained by the various species in their organs is,

of course, determined by their respective environments as well as by the nature of the creatures
with which each species is in correspondence.
The arrangement of these organs amongst one
another is, however, generally the same in all;
there is everywhere expressed the one law of
practicability. The senses are always found in
close proximity to one another; they are outgrowths of one great nerve-center, the brain, and
are invariably situated where their services are
the most needed and where they are the most
efficacious : in the front part of the body, forming
the head. The limbs of the animal have adjusted
themselves preëminently to one kind of exercise,
—the forward motion. This, we see, is determined by the location of the mouth; for the
motion itself is executed by the animal for the
particular purpose of bringing its mouth in contact with articles of food. Thus, the mouth
remains the foremost feature. Then, the air
which the animal is to absorb must be as fresh as
can be obtained; therefore also the breathing
apparatus opens out into the front, at the most
favorable spot. Naturally, the organ of smell is
located within this opening. Here it is to examine the incoming air, not with regard to whole-
someness merely, but also in order to discover the

direction in which the animal must move to find its food. Now, it is not enough that the nose be in front : it must be so situated that it may serve at the same time in the best possible manner in the process of examining the food before this latter is taken into the body. Thus we find the nose always immediately above the mouth. In like manner we may trace the causes for the particular location of eyes and ears. In fact, there is in the animal's body not an organ that has not received its place according to the dictates of the Spirit's clearly defined wisdom. So, for instance, the tail, which, though last, is by no means the least in importance : See how many different uses this appendix must serve in the various species of animals : The pigeon steers its flight with it ; the horse uses it as a protector against injurious insects ; the monkey employs it in climbing ; — we may find many other important services which are rendered by this feature. But its origin, generally speaking, must certainly be the same in all species. Considering that all the perceptive faculties of the animal are located in the fore-part of the body, the rear portion seems comparatively little guarded ; and this circumstance must have furnished the principal motive for the appearance of the appendix. Unconsciously to the animal

itself, the instinctive knowledge of being unable
to keep properly in its view the rear of its body,
must have led the creature to the establishment
of something that might act as a kind of preliminary guard.   So, this tentacle appeared, in order
to serve chiefly the purpose of giving the animal
timely warning of all dangers that threaten in that
immediate vicinity ; the body may thus receive
the necessary attention also in that quarter.

Looking about, we find that many of the species foremost in development have the finest and
largest tails.   See the beautiful tail of the fox,
the Newfoundland dog, the horse, and the long
and nimble tail of the cat, the monkey, etc.; then,
the glory of the peacock, bird of paradise, parrot.

Another proof of the great importance of this
last of the bodily features of the animal is the
fact, that, depriving an animal of its tail, means
destroying its beauty as a creature.   For, what
the eye of one who is in harmony with nature
recognizes anywhere as beauty, is harmony ; and
harmony means that all essentials are present and
active.   When, therefore, a creature appears to
the eye of the correct observer as being in any
respect less beautiful than it was before, we may
know that the former harmony has given place to
a certain discord ; that one or more of the essen-

tial parts of the creature have disappeared; and that, in proportion to how far the creature has lost its beauty, it must have lost also its efficiency.

In every feature distinguishing the animal from the plant we perceive the mighty influence which a life of motion exerts upon the animal-body. Increased perception of danger means improvement of the contrivances for insuring safety. How vastly more active the desire for self-preservation is in the animal than it could ever be in the plant, is shown also in the care which the former bestows upon its offspring. The lowest species, of course, being the weakest of perception, look no more to the welfare of their seed, after this has left them, than does the plant; they content themselves with laying great numbers of eggs. The animals of higher development, for instance, birds, guard their eggs and tend to them until the young come forth; then they transfer their care to the young, until these are able to look out for themselves. These species, therefore, need not and cannot have so great a number of offspring as the former. We are aware that the animals of the species most advanced in the scale of evolution retain their young within themselves, not letting the same appear in the outer world until the organism is so far perfected as to

be in readiness for independent motion. The
nobler the species, the more time and care do the
parents bestow upon their young, and the smaller
is the number produced ; for, the call of necessity
for reproduction in the interest of the preservation of the species limits itself in accordance with
the amount of protection extended towards the
offspring.

We observe still another prominent feature
which distinguishes the animal-body from the
plant : while the latter gives evidence of its inner
life through the substantial vibrations of odor,
the animal-body has, in addition to this kind of
manifestation, acquired power over the more
far-reaching, more penetrating, vibrations of *sound*.
These being of a higher order, the animal has a
far wider range of facility for making itself known.
The sound thus originating within the body by
the volition of the creature is likewise but a
product of the idea of motion : it comes forth as
evidence of the greater activity, the stronger
feeling, within the being.   And, as we are enabled
to discern the character of the harmony within
each plant through the medium of odor, so may
we perceive the inner state of the animal by
taking note of the sound of its voice.   Observe
the difference between the grunt of the pig, the

purring of the cat, the nightingale's song, and the roar of the lion ! Each species of animal has a different idea of the same world; each reflects the conditions of life in accordance with its own power of inner perception. The lion, for instance, in whose make-up the propensity to destroy is powerfully represented, for that reason perceives less of the World's harmony ; and, in consequence, the lion's voice has a less harmonious, less agreeable sound than the voice of the gentler animals, as, for instance, the birds of song. A careful study of the lives and voices of the various animal species will show us that each trait of character exerts its distinct influence upon the character of the voice ; and this latter changes with the degree of activity to which the various propensities are aroused. Thus is called forth the endless variety of sounds expressing the animal's craving and gratification, distress and delight, discord and harmony.

Herewith we have obtained a general view of the powers which the animal-soul has developed in its instrument, the body. Now we will look into the manner in which the soul itself evolves.

CHAPTER VIII.

LIFE OF THE ANIMAL SOUL.

ALTHOUGH the soul equips its body with the various perceptive powers for the purpose of insuring proper guidance in the direction of safety and general well-being, we find that these physical senses cannot be the only means by which the animals obtain their knowledge. We find that these latter are aware of the coming storm, earthquake, volcanic eruption, and other great disturbances in Nature long before any danger can become apparent to the physical senses. We see the swallow returning to the same nest from which it went forth months ago; in the meantime, it has been a thousand miles away from it. A dog will find a lost person, although the animal is guided apparently by nothing but the recollection of the odor of something which that person has worn. It is plain, that the senses of the body cannot reach beyond the physical horizon, nor into the future. Therefore, we see that the powers of the soul are not restricted to acting within the immediate vicinity of the animal, but that the soul perceives also without using the senses of the body ; it has its own peculiar eye, and the instructions coming to the animal through this mode of perception are, as we know, followed implicitly. They are the promptings of what we call the "instinct." This mysterious faculty of seeing through the eye of the soul is, however, not to be regarded as an achievement of the creatures that possess it ; the same is already to be found as an essential feature in the life of the plant. Without this guide it would be utterly impossible to the flower, for instance, to adapt itself so wonderfully to the nature of the visiting insects, and to contrive within the blossom the complicated mechanism that induces these, whether they will or not, to gratify the plant's desire for cross-fertilization with others of its species. The reason why the animal retains its mediumistic quality lies in the fact that the intellect is still comparatively inactive. The power of thought is not yet awakened to such a degree as to conceal original impressions within the animal's mind by covering them with new pictures. Though the creature remains comparatively bare of the more compli-cated knowledge, it continues in perfect harmony with the pure and simple laws which guide its life; and, being constantly under the direct influence of the raw elements, it is only necessary and just, that, whenever circumstances require more knowledge than the animal can obtain through its physical senses, this knowledge should come to the soul directly from the source of Nature herself. Here we are again forcibly reminded of the fact that the soul is not the creation of the brain, but that the latter is created by the soul.

The first qualities brought into play by the soul are, of course, the lowest in the scale; we call them the "animal propensities." As we have already noted, the foremost of these is the desire for acquisition of substance: the animal wants to eat and drink to sustain its life; therefore it must provide for itself the necessary substance. Now, in the animal-world the conditions for obtaining the required nourishment are not always favorable. Thus we see the animals compelled to lay up stores of food and to hide the same away. The faculty which prompts and enables them to do this, we know by the term "secretiveness." We have seen also that the desire for self-preservation forces each animal into an attitude of aggressiveness towards its fellow-creatures; it is compelled, both to fight and to defend itself; it exercises, in addition to the former faculties, also those of combativeness, destructiveness, firmness and caution.

We observe, that, next to the desire for preservation of self, the mightiest impulse in the animal is that for the maintenance of the species. As the degree of consciousness increases, we find the animal more sensible, not alone to the dangers besetting its individual being, but also of those which menace its offspring. The animal finds it necessary to extend its care for individual safety and well-being also to its young; its desire for maintenance of the species evolves into love for the particular young which it brings forth; it provides for its offspring. A secluded place must be found where they may be raised in safety; a *home* is established, and the parents are impelled to continue in each other's company. While the female attends to her duties as mother, protecting the young and watching over the home, her mate provides the food and protects the whole establishment. Thus are evolved the faculties of inhabitiveness, continuity, and conjugal love.

With many animals, the establishment of a home means the building of one; birds must build their nests; foxes, spiders, etc., must all construct

their respective abodes. Thus we see the intellectual faculties of constructiveness, ideality, and
imitation come forth in active demonstration. In
fact, when we look more carefully into the lives
of the various animals, we become aware that
each faculty of the intellect is here represented in
some one or more species, to the degree determined by the relations existing between the species and their surroundings. We find that the
senses of locality, tune, and time, the facility for
observing size, form, color, weight, for perceiving
the order of things, comparing these with one
another, and remembering both objects and the
events connected with the same, — are all present. Even the highest of the intellectual powers,
that of tracing cause and effect, is not missing;
for there is abundant evidence that this faculty,
too, here and there comes forth and helps the
animal. These powers are, of course, all evolved
direct through the medium of the various physical
senses.

Here our attention is arrested by an additional
feature: We have observed that the animal has
obtained power over the vibrations of sound.
Now, as the creature moves about, it cannot
always remain in line of vision with its companions. Family-life, for instance, demands that the

animals be constantly informed of one another's whereabouts. Where this information cannot be obtained through the power of vision, some other means must be resorted to. Thus, as a substitute, the sense of hearing is placed in correspondence with the powers of the voice : certain sounds are, by instinctive and mutual understanding, connected with certain meanings ; the animals receive intelligence from each other without the aid of vision ; they cultivate this means of communication, and thus originates the power of speech.

There are as many different environments as there are species of animals to live in them ; and, as we see, the general development of each animal corresponds with the position which the creature occupies in the World. The fox, for instance, which preys chiefly upon birds and other nimble animals, must continually exercise an extraordinary degree of cunning. The swallow, which must travel to and fro between its little home in the north and the far off southern countries, has a correspondingly strong development of the sense of locality. The spider is known for its great ingenuity in contriving and constructing. Each of the propensities, the selfish as well as the social, and each intellectual faculty, is thus particularly emphasized above the others in some one or more species.

We observe that the animals of many species have not extended their consideration to the family-life merely, but that their whole families unite in herds and flocks. Of course, this union forms itself within the species only. The desire for this mode of living arises from the individual's instinctive perception of its weakness as compared with the power of the enemy. We see even wolves combine against the stronger creature. This tendency is, however, in many cases also an evidence of higher development of soul. We observe that elephants, monkeys, — many species of animals of a high nature, — likewise travel in herds. Let us direct our attention to those of the latter class : These, we find, are drawn into one another's society, not alone through the instinctive knowledge that greater safety is obtained through life in union with others of their kind, but they show that they cultivate this sociability also for its own sake. This is the primitive expression of the faculty of friendship. They recognize one another as being of the like nature and as being placed in the like relationship to the animals of other species. Their natures being so perfectly similar that each sees itself reflected in those of its kind, they all-together practically join to represent but one soul, the dictates of which being implicitly obeyed by each individual. Thus we see the first appearance of organization among separate full-grown creatures. One of the herd is elevated to the position of leader and guardian of all the rest. This animal now looks after the welfare of its companions, and, in return, receives their acknowledgement of its superiority; for they follow and obey. In the ability of the animal to recognize a leader we note the first indication of the presence of moral sentiment in the animal-world; we observe the primitive expression of the faculty of veneration. The holding of a position of superiority implies the presence of the feeling of confidence in self as well as firmness of will; while the responsibility attending this position of trust necessitates conscientiousness in the leader as well as in the herd which is to follow him. Where there is difference in station, there is also a certain degree of ambition. We further note, that, in extending his attention beyond his own immediate interests to those of the whole herd, or flock, the leader gives evidence of an inclination, however faint, towards the exercise of benevolence. As his companions perceive the benefit obtained in consequence of his leader-

ship, they become disposed to the feeling of confidence, faith, — the twin-sister of hope. We
may make these observations while watching, for
instance, the chickens : see how the rooster provides for his wards, how he calls them when he
has made a lucky find, and how these gather con-
fidingly around him.

How far the highest faculties of the soul, the
powers of moral judgment, are developed in the
animal-world, may be particularly observed in the
social life of such as elephants and monkeys,
which hold veritable courts of justice : an individual has been accused of violating one of the
important laws of the community ; there is a
general meeting ; judge, accuser, and defence, —
all are present ; evidence is taken ; and then,
after an excited controversy, when the culprit has
been judged guilty, he is forthwith expelled from
the herd, which thereupon leaves the place. He
follows at a distance, crying in his distress ; —
he had *hoped* to be acquitted.

Thus we see, that, in the animal world, not
only all the selfish, social, and intellectual faculties are represented, but also every one of the
moral sentiments ; — each one with special force
in some particular species. How would this
social life which we observe among the more

highly developed animals be possible, if they had not moral perception? For, the higher sentiments are really nothing else than the perception of the laws which bring forth and sustain a community.

But now the question arises within us, " If the animal-world possesses all the faculties which characterize the human being, — why, then, does neither the social, nor the individual condition of the animals admit of any further evolution?" We see, that, as a plant must ever remain a plant, so an elephant remains an elephant, a dog can never be aught but a dog, and so forth; each animal, no matter how highly it evolves its faculties, is still restricted to its original nature, — ever remaining but an animal. Evolution has once more reached a limit.   Why?   .

We observed, while contemplating the life of the plant, how the limit of evolution on that plane is determined by the manner in which the plant obeys the impulse of self-preservation.   We saw, that, in the plants, further evolution is impossible by reason of their nature as beings without the power of independent motion; and that the higher life comes into existence only through giving to the creature this power and also the nature to make use of it.   Now let us take a view in

general outline of the conditions prevailing among
the animals : We have seen how each species
is differently constituted from the very start.
While the plant-species, in their tranquil, stationary existence, represent the various traits of character in the form merely of reflections, and
pictures, or symbols; we find the animals, by
reason of the higher consciousness resulting
from their life of motion, able to demonstrate
these traits as living realities. Each kind of animal represents certain traits of character as they
appear in active form, in life; but not a single
animal ever proceeds to develop within itself any
of the faculties in which the other species excel.
Each species restricts itself to those characteristics with which it happens to be favored from the
beginning, and· can rise no further in the scale of
life and power. Why ? Because there is no possibility of any perfect coöperation among the
various species. Neither of them is qualified for
forming such a union with other species as would
be required for the transmission of powers from
one to the other. The souls representing the
various species of animals, notwithstanding the
fact that they are of the same Spirit and permeated with the like general motive, are as different
from one another as are their bodies. Being so

vastly different, and at the same time so powerfully prompted to assert their respective individu-
alities at one another's expense, these species
remain blind to one another's inner natures, and
can thus never become cognizant of advantages
contained in traits which they themselves do not
already possess.   Each animal, therefore, remains
content with strictly adapting itself to the sphere
in which it came forth; because, under the circumstances, departure from the same would result
in the destruction of the creature.   The animal,
like the plant, may make its own individuality
more pronounced; but that is all.

Thus we see that the cause which bars the
further evolution of life on the animal plane is
similar to that through which the powers of the
plant are limited: As the plant continues a solitary
being upon its piece of earth, so the animal-soul
remains fixed within the solitude of its particular
species.   Further evolution of life is possible
only through the introduction of more freedom,
more independence of motion.   But this requires
the establishment of more harmony.   Now, it is
plain that the conditions existent in the animal-
world are there to stay; that the animal-species,
by their very constitution, are forced to continue
alternately preying upon one another and getting

out of one another's way. The spiritual atmosphere of their world can never change ; they
know of none other, and it is impossible for any
of them to rise out of its twilight into a brighter
and larger sphere of existence. The spark of
life within them is not powerful enough to show
them that there is a way beyond. Not even
those animals which live in the more peaceful and
harmonious circumstances surroundiug the human
family, can understand the higher life sufficiently
to grow into the same. The noble dog, for
instance, although it has evolved some of the
highest faculties, such as veneration and faithfulness, to a degree of power not exceeded in the
human, still remains within its own sphere, by
natural preference. This creature will sacrifice
its life for man, but it cannot see far enough into
the nature of human existence to prefer the same
to its own. The life of man is to the dog as
incomprehensible and inimitable as the life of a
divine being is to man. The dog may extend its
benevolence also to a cat, but it sees no reason
for adopting any of the likes and dislikes, and
faculties in general, which characterize the object
of its attentions. The animal's soul and body
have perfectly adapted themselves to the life
which it wants to lead, and so the species remains

intact in all its characteristics. Thus we see why the further evolution of life is dependent upon the introduction of a new idea.

CHAPTER IX.

FORMATION AND NATURE OF THE HUMAN BODY.

THE Law says, "More harmony, more freedom, — greater development." The Law must be complied with. All the evidence before our eyes shows us that there is but one process possible by which this greater harmony may be established; and this process consists in uniting a variety of animal-souls and compelling them to live together in a common body, so that they may be dependent solely upon this for all their manifestations. Each of these animal-species must join its characteristics with those of the others, and likewise must this body be equipped with such structural features as are required for the gratification of each of the traits and faculties represented. So that this union may be possible, these souls must all derive their growth out of one and the same spiritual root, that is, they must be united through singleness of motive. We know that this motive is already present; it is the same, which, in the animal-world, causes the species to remain separated and thus to be barred from further development : it is the old desire for preservation of self and kind. Now, when these various souls find themselves inseparably united in one body, this common desire becomes the very motive which must insure their coöperation; for this joint body is the only one in their possession. In fact, the voices of the many being combined, the anxiety for the preservation of this body is only so much the stronger. On this fundamental principle, then, is established the combined activity of all. Each soul is now bound to help the others, in order to maintain itself. This condition being fulfilled, each is free to follow its own impulse towards individual, social, and moral activity, aided by the combined intellectual powers of all.

Let us look first at the general nature of this body : It is plain that that soul which contains the various faculties in the most harmonious proportion is represented in the animal-world by the most perfectly equipped body. The structure of this body, inasmuch as it is the one which would answer most nearly the requirements of the souls of the other species when united, will thus become the model for the construction of the common body. This most perfect of the animal-bodies is, as we are aware, that of the monkey; it has the most manifold facility for motion; it is the most nimble; while in the construction of the hand, as possessed by none of the other animals, we recognize the powerful medium with the help of which life may establish itself on the higher plane. According to the proportions in which the various species are to be represented in the common body, will its features be modified, so as to meet more perfectly the requirements of each ; but, as we observe, its general configuration remains the same in every instance. In its features we shall always find expressed the same superiority over the bodies of the individual animals; it is ever recognizable as the representative of the one grand species established on a higher plane of life, — the *human*.

We find in this body the requisites for absorption and assimilation of all the various kinds of food, animal as well as vegetable; each animal is represented in the character of teeth and stomach. Feet and hands, both are present. The united perceptive powers of the different species has naturally brought forth an harmonious development of the physical senses which are to serve them all. Thus, the senses of feeling, taste, and smell understand at once the nature of all the substances with which the individual animals are in correspondence.   The ear responds to a range of sound-vibrations such as will satisfy the needs of all species, while the eye can perceive all colors and forms.   Each animal brings, together with the trait peculiar to itself, also the character of voice determined by the same.   Thus, in the human body, the voice not only has the power of expressing each trait separately, but, as these are all united in the same, this voice is far superior to that of any one of the animal-voices with respect to character in general.

When we observe the shape, size, and quality of the brain which governs the body, the result of the blending of these various animal-souls into one is shown to us most clearly.   Each trait is here represented by its organic substance.   All the animal propensities are present in superior strength and proportion : The desire for food has at its disposal in the brain an organ manifold enough to gratify the tastes of each species. The impulse towards reproduction, which in each kind of animal is active at a different time of the year, is, because of their union within the human body, capable of appearance at any time the year round ; thus each is gratified.   Likewise is the character of parental-love of a superior strength and quality. So are also the faculties of acquisitiveness, secretiveness, caution, and so forth, each increased in power through the union of these souls. The same may be observed with regard to all the higher organs; the social, moral, and intellectual; the traits of fox, pig, crow, and cat may be found living together in the same body with those of the sheep, elephant, dog, and monkey; making themselves recognizable according to their prominence, not alone within the person, but likewise in his exterior, especially in the face.

Also is the human body finer in texture than that of any animal: increased complexity of mind demands and produces a finer cerebral structure, and this, in turn, forms a superior nervous system throughout the body, refining the various organs through increasing their sensibility. Thus also is the human skin, where these finer nerves terminate, rendered more susceptible, more delicate.

Now, however, we perceive that there are some prominent features of the animal-body not present in the human: there are neither fins, wings, nor tail. Why are these missing? Respecting the first named, we know that these serve the fish as propellers merely, adjusted to the nature of the element in which it lives. The limbs of the human body enable this to move through the same element; but this body is not designed for life within the same; nor is it endowed with independent powers of locomotion through the atmosphere; — it is restricted to life on the solid soil. Why? We find that the animals living on land are more complex in the development of their faculties; they are more powerful of influence than either fish or fowl. Therefore they have the controlling power in the choice of the element which is to be the home of the common body. They determine the body with respect also to its form: Four limbs is the number required by the higher species of animal as well as by the bird. Two of these limbs must be legs with feet, the other two, arms with hands; this is the result of the compromise between the monkey and these other animals. The fish, being by reason of their weaker life in the darker element, the lowest in the scale, are, of course, represented accordingly; still, this body has at least some little facility for moving in their element. The birds, however, are, so far as their peculiar mode of locomotion is concerned, not considered at all; the human body, like their own, moves about on two feet, and in their element; but independent rising above the ground is denied. We may find a rea-

son for this : When we examine the nature and
life of the bird in general, we observe that the
power of flight is, in itself, not so much an object
of the animal's desire as at first glance appears.
Its body being lighter, and therefore weaker of
resistance than those of other animals, the bird is
not alone impelled, but also empowered, to make
itself less easily approachable ; and the way in
which it does this, is by making itself independent of a hold upon the ground, so that it may at
any time get beyond the reach of the heavier
animals by rising into the air.   The faculties
of the bird-soul are not awakened to such a
degree that it desires the power of flight for pleasures such as this manner of motion would contain
for us.   The bird does not care for the beautiful
and sublime in scenery as we do ; nor does it
appreciate much the swiftness of its flight.   The
swiftness of the bird is caused by the nature of
its body and environment.   How little the animal
cares for the pleasures to be found in this kind of
motion, is evidenced by the generally low degree
of development in the uncultivated human being
of the faculty of sublimity.   The desire for
expressing itself through the medium of song
is, perhaps, the principal distinguishing feature
by which the bird-nature is represented in the

human ; and the organs required for the gratification of this desire, the sense of music, are present accordingly. We find that the bird really has no impulses which may not be gratified by the human body in its present form ; thus the power of flight is denied to this body for the reason merely that on the human plane of life there has as yet been no general call of necessity for that faculty.

Now remains the question, "Why is that, which, in the animal, is so important a feature, namely, the tail, not present?" Here also we may find the answer while observing the reason why there is no necessity for the same. We know that in the animal-world the tail serves pre-eminently as guard and protector in otherwise neglected parts. Now, the human body, by reason of its vertical position, is never so exposed in the back parts as the animal. Besides, the human head is more favorably situated for quickly turning about in all directions. In addition to these advantages, the mind within has the power and the organs for contriving all manner of artificial guard and defense, which are denied to the animal. We can thus find no cause whatever for the presence of such a feature on the human form. The tail remains excluded from the same through the absence of a call of necessity ; and where such a feature should ever apparently come forth on human beings, it could be only in the form of a so-called freak of Nature, not constructed in accordance with the distinctive qualities of the real tail, and therefore not to be considered as being one.

Having thus made ourselves acquainted with the general character of the human body, we will now turn our attention to the soul.

CHAPTER X.

CONSTITUTION OF THE HUMAN SOUL; ORIGIN
OF THE RACES.

THUS far we have observed but the separate elements of life; we have, so to speak, studied the great language of the Spirit with reference merely to its alphabet and vocabulary. Is the human soul great enough to understand its own existence? — to read the thoughts expressed by the Spirit on the high plane of human life? Let us try.

Before we proceed, however, to enter this higher sphere, a most important question occurs to us, "Does the Spirit, while blending the animal-souls to form the human, add anything to the character of their life-vibration, or is this brighter spark of life entirely the result of this union?" Our personal sense can never tell us; for the question touches upon the soul's innermost nature. We must attempt a view through the eye of the Spirit: While observing the manner in which the primitive stage of life originates,

we saw how the various elementary substances
are combined through the medium of the sun-
beam into a variety of organisms. In thus uniting these elements and permeating them with its
life the Spirit gives to them a signification, somewhat as we, through forming words, give sense to
the letters of our alphabet. Each of these organisms on the vegetable plane, as we have seen, is
the symbol of a certain trait of character, — the
reflection of a "word." The Spirit introduces
into these mere pictures of character the idea of
motion : they come to life in the life of the animal ; — thus the Spirit's ideal "words" become
realities. Then we saw how these traits must
remain separated from one another in the various
species. However, they are all of the same great
Spirit, which has created them for a certain higher
purpose : As we form our words for the special
purpose of using them in our sentences ; so does
the Spirit give separate life to the various traits
of character, in order that it may form combinations of them for expression of its higher, more
complicated ideas on the plane of human life.
We know that the thoughts which we desire to
express in our sentences, require for their appearance as realities nothing more than that the words
forming these sentences be well chosen and

placed in their proper order. We may suppose that likewise the Spirit demonstrates its ideas in the form of human life without putting anything further into the combinations which it makes of the various animal-souls, than the force of the ideas themselves. That which effects and maintains these combinations, we have already recognized as being the desire of the Spirit for superior harmony.

In looking about in the world of human beings, we see that these are divided into a number of different species, or races. Did these originally come forth out of one family and in one locality, or, like the various plant and animal species, from different germs and in different countries?

Upon closer observation of the life on the lower planes we find that a vast number of plant and animal species ever remain confined to certain localities, — so strictly so that, if they were placed in environments of a nature different from that of their own, they would die out. The reason is, of course, to be found in the marked differences maintained between the various regions with respect to climate, character of soil, and the many other conditions in the midst of which the organisms find their birth and means of sustenance. It is quite evident that each species can have made its first appearance in that kind of locality alone to which it remains thus confined. Now, in observing the manner in which the human races are distributed over the Earth, we note that during these many ages they, too, have remained each established in a region of its own as firmly almost as a plant remains rooted to its piece of soil. For thousands of years there has been comparatively little mingling among them. Although races may spread beyond the limits of their respective countries, each nevertheless still holds dear the land in which it passed its childhood. It appears, moreover, that even with a perfect intermingling of the races an amalgamation into one could never come about, by reason of the too pronounced difference between their physical characteristics. Each race, like the individual creature, lives its allotted time and then passes away. Thus, in the course of evolution a multitude of races in all regions have succeeded one another, each in turn eventually giving up its home on Earth to another that was at the time possessed of greater vitality.

Now, we see that the body of man contains the same earthly substance as that of animal and plant ; it is therefore also subject to the same law. Thus we may be justified in taking for granted that, as the difference existing between the natures of the various localities at the time of the first appearance of Life caused a separate coming-forth of various plant and animal species, so likewise the human life made its first appearance on Earth in the form of a variety of races, each coming forth independently of the others, in a different locality, and from a different germ.

Difference in body, as we know, means difference in soul; and, indeed, our races differ widely as to the character of soul in the individuals representing them. Let us make a few observations bearing upon this point: Consider, for instance, the mental constitution of the average Negro in his original state. The proportions in which his faculties stand to one another show as plainly in the shape of his head, and in the form and expression of his features, as they do in his manner of life. By far the larger part of his brain lies in the back part of his head. His propensities, all strongly present, are preëminently under the influence of the social feelings. Sociability, being the strongest of his higher impulses, therefore determines the nature of his whole existence. He delights in the society of his fellows, because he has a strong instinctive perception of the pleasures arising from harmonious intercourse. Perceiving and cultivating harmony is, as we are aware, equivalent to cultivating a happy disposition, a light heart. The Negro certainly has this, and he shows it in the expression of his face. The state of the soul determines not only the tone of the voice, but also the activity of the faculties pertaining to music; and thus we find the Negro generally to be the possessor of an agreeable voice combined with high musical ability. All the faculties which are the immediate outgrowths of social life are, in the Negro, well developed. The desire to venerate, the love of praise, suavity, mirthfulness, the faculties of imitation, faith, hope, memory, and the power of language, — all these are prominent characteristics; while, on the other hand, in the faculties which grow out of a life more laborious, more devoted to stern duty, he proves in many respects to be deficient.

Entirely different proportions do we find in the original North American Indian. The head of the latter is less developed in the region of the social organs; but, instead, it is broader in the purely selfish propensities, higher in the back part of the crown, and fuller in the region of the intellect. His propensities are less dominated by the social faculties than are those of the Negro; he perceives less of harmony; his greater destructiveness, firmness and self-esteem make of him a sterner being. In consequence, the expression on his face is that of severity. In his mind, mirthfulness and music find little room. Being more secretive, more self-contained, he has less use also for the power of language. His life being more laborious than that of the Negro, his intellectual faculties in general are more strongly developed than are those of the latter. All in all, the Indian is more conscious of self and, at the same time, less happy.

A more perfect proportion in the development of the faculties is to be found in the Malayan, and especially in the Mongolian race. Both of these show a higher moral as well as intellectual power. The Malayan, by reason of living in a warmer, friendlier climate, possesses a more careless disposition than we find in the Mongolian, who is forced by the severer climate to labor. But the same conditions which require a higher mental activity, also help to generate the strength for its endurance : alternation between warm and cold seasons invigorates the nervous system. Thus, the Mongolian is superior to the Malayan as well as to the other two races.

We have now to consider the race most advanced of all, the Caucasian. This, we find,

distinguishes itself from the rest through representing the greatest variety of characters.   It is
the most complicated of the Spirit's expressions
in the form of man.   In this race are united all
the mental characteristics in as high a degree of
development as that in which they are to be found
separately in each of the others ; and therefore it
is qualified for attaining, with respect both to its
individual members and to the race as a body,
the highest degree of evolution possible to man
on Earth.   For this reason, and because this is
the race to which our personalities belong, we
will make its life the prominent object of our
attention.

CHAPTER XI.

WE find here every possible trait of character, from the lowest to the highest, personated by some one or more individuals. No two souls are alike, and no two physical bodies. According to which of the animal-souls in each case predominates, may we recognize in the personal features and general bearing the character of dog or cat, hog or fox, goose or eagle, and so on through the line. One of the factors most generally represented is, for instance, the dog-soul. This is evidenced, not alone in the friendly feelings between man and dog, but also in the opposite, in cases of hydrophobia: Though a man be not even touched by the dog, still it will happen that he develops all the symptoms of the dog's disease; barking and snapping like the dog itself. It is plain that this man could not, in his unconscious condition, so perfectly imitate the animal, if the dog-soul were not present within himself. This dog-soul in the human required merely to be aroused by the kind of incident which, in its life on the higher plane, so strongly appeals to its sympathies. It then, for the time being, becomes in a certain respect disconnected from its union with the other souls, and thus its excitement brings it into fearful prominence.

We have already, while studying the animal-world, seen how the various faculties originally came into life, and how their further evolution on that plane is arrested by reason of their isolation in the different species. Here, in the human world, we see the faculties united in the bodies and free to intermingle. We note that the human soul, even in its primitive stages of development, is vastly more conscious of existence than is the animal; for, the impulse towards self-preservation existent in the various animal-souls has become united in one soul, and this increased love of life now calls for a greater activity among all the higher faculties. They must now all exert themselves in the interest of a common cause: the preservation of life in human form. We will observe how they help man in his efforts to rise out of the primitive stage in which he first makes his appearance.

By reason of his higher nature, he comes forth in the bosom of the family. However, he perceives himself surrounded, like the beings on the plane below, by every kind of enemy, beasts of prey, and many other influences hostile to his existence. But he also finds in close vicinity, besides the members of his family, other fellow-beings of the same nature as his own ; and, in obedience to the law of affinity, he combines with these against the common enemy. Thus, several families together form a primitive society, a tribe, placing themselves under the guardianship of a chief. Now the intellect calls the hands to work: homes are constructed. The body of man, being weaker than that of the animal, must be provided with artificial means of both attack and defense ; the effect of a blow is increased through adding to the swing of the arm the length of a stick, a club, with the heaviest end toward the enemy. The tender skin is protected by a piece from the hide of an animal. Then follows the discovery that better success is attainable through making of this hide a shield, and thus employing simulta-neously one arm in the attack and the other in the defense. The combined intellect observes the effects, remembers experiences, analyzes facts, reconstructs their relations to one another, and so arrives at the conception of new ideas. Thus, the next in line is the discovery of means by which to kill the enemy from a distance; spears, and bows and arrows are invented. The safety of his existence becoming more and more firmly established, man's attention is now attracted also toward bodily comforts; the hands find employment in the manufacture of various household articles; materials are found which suggest to him the idea of woven dress. The skillfulness of the hands, through exercise, grows in step with the power of the intellect to perceive and to contrive. Each invention gives rise to another, and the hands are ready to materialize the idea. The refinement of the intellectual powers enables him to perceive certain harmonies in the surrounding World which remain hidden to the senses of the animal; and as the skill of his hands grows more perfect, he begins to give expression to the pleasure which he receives from these finer perceptions, by imitating the beauties of Nature in his works: he embellishes that which he makes, and forms images. He gradually becomes acquainted also with the laws that govern the harmony of sound. From merely imitating Nature's harmonies, he proceeds to place them in new relationships with one another; he creates new forms, and thus his powers of invention find their expression also in the various branches of art.

While the mind is thus employed in securing safety and comfort to the body, and providing all manner of enjoyments for the senses, it must likewise see to the safety of the articles thus produced. The natural result is, that the primitive laws, such as we find governing the herds and flocks in the animal-world, are, in this human society, extended beyond the individual to the protection of his personal property. Each of these individuals desires to enjoy the fruits of his labors in person. Perceiving the wholesome effect of the laws which secure protection to himself and his family, he feels encouraged to come to a mutual understanding with his fellows in regard to all his other belongings. The more harmony there is in a community, the more security for each member. Thus, each pledges himself to respect the property of his fellows, and to recognize the justice of all penalties attached to transgressions ; each member himself helps to make the law. In this manner is awakened to higher activity the sense of conscientiousness. Now, where there is law, there must be also a power to guard and execute the same : certain individuals are chosen to act as officers under the chief ; they are vested with authority over others. Thus is nourished the faculty of ambition.

As the community grows and as its individual harmony, as well as that with other communities, becomes more and more firmly established, we see the supreme authority more and more generally accorded to the body of moral sentiments: the finer voice is heard above the coarser. Meanwhile the intellect continues in its occupation of contriving new and better employment for the hands; and each generation transmits to the following one the powers thus evolved. In consequence, also the amount of property grows, and, by reason of the inequality in the development of the individuals, becomes unevenly divided. Thus, from generation to generation the manifold contrasts between the inner and outer conditions of the several families become more marked, and distinct classes form, the various families slowly, or sometimes suddenly, moving from one class of life into the other. This manifold change of contrasts, this condition of perpetual motion, has the effect of still more enlivening both the intellectual faculties and the moral sentiments of all concerned. Care and lightness of heart, melancholy and mirthfulness, come to the individual in manifold degree and form. Thus, the high sentiments of faith and hope and charity, which are the great harmonizers in the human world, receive abun-

dant opportunities for coming forth to demonstrate the natural brotherhood of all mankind.
Finally, as all the faculties become more and more
awake to the true nature of existence, learning to
distinguish the changeable from the unchange-
able, the personal from the universal, man gradually becomes aware of that to which he owes his
reverence. He begins to sense more clearly the
presence of the Spirit, the Father of all, and so
his faculty of veneration, which, at first, could
address itself to the personal, the perishable, only,
now becomes empowered to help him rise into
conscious communication with the eternal, the
Creator himself.

In taking a general view of the manner in
which the faculties evolve on the human plane,
we observe that their unfoldment is effected
chiefly by means of the communication which
they establish among the individual souls. They
learn to communicate, not alone through the
medium of language and material contrivances,
but likewise through the direct action of soul
upon soul. While the plant gives evidence of its
being through its vibrations of odor, and the
animal has acquired power over those of sound,
the human being learns to command the fine
vibrations of thought and feeling. Our study of

the life on the lower planes has shown us that
the soul of plant and animal reaches beyond
the body and receives impressions. Man's soul
acquires the power, not only of receiving knowledge in this manner, but also of impressing its
thought upon others, independently of distance
and physical means. This power of thought-
transference has evolved in the human world as a
result of the higher activity and the more complicated harmony existing among the various individual souls. There is present, not alone the
desire to receive, but also the will to impress.
We may compare the human beings in this respect
to the stringed instruments : each instrument
transmits its vibrations to every one of the others
which is within reach of the sound-vibrations and
harmonizes with the same. Now, we have seen
that the soul is independent of both locality and
substance. Therefore, in so far as there exists a
likeness, or an affinity, between souls, however
far their bodies may be apart, the vibrations of
each of these souls will immediately be felt by
the others also. Where the power of will is
strong in one, and the receptivity great in another,
there we may find taking place a transmission of
thought and feeling, effected alone by the power
of will. We see that this transmission often

proves to be so perfect as to excite to action the physical senses of the recipient: it happens that persons make themselves unexpectedly apparent to the eye and ear, and senses in general, of others who are at that moment thousands of miles away.

We further observe that the power of soul-vibration is not alone thus independent of substance, but that it may even temporarily alter the relations between objects, as, for instance, the hypnotizer does when, by mere will-power, he invests weak objects with superior strength, and in the same way increases or reduces their weight. It is plain that from such a changing of relations between substances to the feat of combining these to form new objects, also by direct soul-power, is only a step. The Universe consisting in nothing but vibrations, the soul acquires its power over mind and matter through bringing its own vibrative force into a certain harmony with that upon which it wants to act; its power evolves solely through this kind of effort. Everywhere we find expressed the necessity of harmonious action. The Spirit demonstrates this to us on every plane of existence. Each higher plane comes forth through the introduction of an idea designed to increase the harmonious intercourse of forces. Thus we have seen how the life in each higher sphere becomes more complicated, more pronounced, more powerful, as the forces of the lower faculties become more closely united with those of the higher, forming with these a better harmony, through which they are lifted out of the lower plane to serve on the higher. As the lower faculties constitute the impulse of self-preservation, we readily understand why the unfoldment of life remains so strictly conditioned upon the evolution of this impulse. And each plane stands as a well-defined creation, although dependent for its existence upon those below, yet, within itself, remaining forever intact. In each we may find reflected in a certain form the likeness of all; for we can find in the Universe no two things that do not in some respect allow comparison. In this we are shown how they alltogether are the emanations of but the one Spirit, which brings them forth for one another to form one harmonious being. As we look, for instance, upon the manifold life on our human plane, as shown in a civilized community, and observe the innumerable forms of individual occupation, from that of mere manual labor to that of invention and art, from that of distributing the goods of Earth to that of dispensing the heavenly; as we see how the community thus provides itself with its requirements from all directions, below and above, gathering-in both the material and the spiritual, we truly find reflected there the harmonious life of the blooming plant: There are the roots, which secure the earthly substance ; this is, through the stem, conveyed into all the different parts ; while the leaves must help to insure a healthy development.   Thus invigorated and purified, the plant may then evolve its beautiful flower.   This, in turn, unfolding toward the Sun, drinks in the rays of light and warmth ; and as this blossom imparts their life to the seed within its care, the plant becomes enabled to insure the maintenance and further evolution of its species.

Having, by means of the observations so far made, obtained an idea of the manner in which our Earth evolves the faculties from their symbolical appearance in the plant to their life in the human-being, let us now take a step nearer and observe the fate which they bring to the individual creature.

CHAPTER XII.

FATE, WITH REGARD TO PLANT AND ANIMAL.

OUR observations have shown us that all the various forms of life with which we are surrounded are, so to speak, a spectrum of the Spirit, appearing upon the surface of the Earth as a refraction of the Sun's rays through planetary substance. We have seen that the great Spirit, by itself, is but the Principle, the Law; and that the world of souls is the demonstration of its being. The Spirit appears as the one great Law of life; and life, as we know, is but another word for feeling. Thus we are aware that the one and only object of the Spirit consists in the *evolution of feeling*. This latter, therefore, must form the central object of our present attention.

We find, while looking into the activity on the first stage of soul-existence, the vegetable plane, that, in the plant, consciousness of life, or feeling, can not much exceed that degree which is necessary for impelling the creature to maintain merely the life of itself and its species. However, the various movements within the body of the plant must surely be accompanied by pleasurable feelings to some degree, be they ever so instinct-ive. What else would induce, for instance, the germ of the rose to drive a root into the ground, and at the same time to send a shoot out of the darkness through the solid earth above? what could impel it to the effort of overcoming the great law of gravitation so as to reach the day-light, if it be not the instinctive knowledge that its wants shall be gratified when it succeeds? When, at last, the Sun opens the buds which it turns up to him, the sweet odor of its blossom is surely recognizable as an evidence of a certain feeling of gratification pervading the plant. The soul of the plant is, however, still a very weak one. The plant can retain within its own body but a small portion of the life-vibrations coming to it; the rest must be provided with separate bodies. Thus we see it contrive all the require-ments for the process of reproduction; it would not do this, if there were not a desire present; and desire implies feeling.

But now we see that the tranquil life of the plant is not all gratification; we see great num-bers maimed and destroyed. The plant is subject to the desire of the higher creatures as well as to the destructive influence of the elements; and thus, where gratification brought pleasure, the reverse produces pain. As much capacity as there is for the one kind of sensation, will there, of course, also be for the other. However small this sensation may seem to be to us, still, the plant feels it; and here a question arises in our minds, "Why should a harmless plant, even though it be only a plant, meet with an adverse fate and come to grief, — and why is a distinction made, by which some are left to grow in size and beauty, and eventually to die the peaceful death of ripe old age, while to others all this is denied?" Nature must certainly contain an answer to this question somewhere; for the Spirit must be as just as it is strict.

We will proceed, and look into the fate of the animal: Where there is more life, there is also more to lose. The animal, being more conscious of its existence, makes greater efforts at preserving the same. Its life being more manifold, it experiences more desires, has more power of feeling. In the lower species there can, of course, be little difference between the feeling of an animal and that of a plant. Power of feeling, as we know, increases with development of soul. And see what contrasts are to be found between

pleasure and pain among the higher species!
Here, where the desire for self-preservation is
sufficiently pronounced to show clearly the separate promptings of all its elements, namely, the
propensities, we may observe how the power of
feeling becomes diversified.   The life of the moving creature causes suddenness as well as variety
of experience : the propensities are impelled to
separate activity.   Of the desires to eat, drink,
reproduce, etc., each has its time of gratification
apart from that of the others : The lion prowls
about for prey ; he is moved by a desire.   Coming
upon an animal, he enters a fight, and his propensity to destroy becomes gratified.   Rejoicing
in his own grim way, he brings his victim to his
mate and young, which are waiting for it in his
cave ; then the cravings for food are stilled; and
that done, there may follow a period of rest and
enjoyment in the home circle.

But, as we know, it may just as easily come
otherwise; the animal is subject to the desires of
others as well as to its own.   Thus it happens
that this lion loses his mate and cubs; that he
himself is wounded, deprived of his home and
wonted liberty ; or, he may be destroyed by violence.   His pain must at such times be as great
as were his pleasurable feelings during the periods

of good fortune ; and the indulgence of his various bodily impulses was, after all, in vain. Like
the plant, he comes to grief. From general
observation we come to the conclusion that the
feelings which have their source in the animal's
concern for self and kind, though pleasurable to
the creature at the moments of their gratification,
are otherwise always painful, and always ready to
assume the character of instinctive, though well-
grounded, fear that somehow there will be enforced
a payment for these various enjoyments which are
had at foreign expense.

How is it with regard to the feelings arising
from the higher faculties, the affections reaching
beyond the animal's personality and species?
Let us consider, for instance, the feelings of the
dog : This creature lives in an environment somewhat removed from the dangers which generally
threaten the world of animals; it is relieved of
much of the anxiety which prevails there concerning the preservation of the body. Its interest is therefore permitted in a degree to go out
into the life surrounding, to manifest itself in the
nature of sociability : the dog cultivates friend-
ships with animals of other species. The natural
development of its higher faculties, however,
attracts it with superior power to the sphere of

man; and, moreover, instinctively recognizing how prominently the soul of its own kind is represented in the human being, all its higher feelings concentrate around its relationship with him. Leaving out of consideration the lower feelings, which it shares with all the other animals, we will observe those derived from its higher faculties alone. That which so firmly binds the soul of the noble dog to that of man is, as we see, the sentiment of veneration. The dog's instinctive perception of the superiority of the human nature to its own, together with its strong desire for cultivating friendliness in superior quarters, leads it to regard man, not only as the superior being, but likewise as the trustworthy friend. Its confidence expresses itself in its reverence. How otherwise could it, notwithstanding its oftentimes far superior strength, so patiently endure painful abuses heaped upon it by the objects of its worship? We see that in the consideration of the dog the bodily force of the human being has comparatively little part; for the animal often voluntarily obeys the child, while disregarding the authority of the man. The animal makes such clear distinctions between likes and dislikes, that, if we did not already know that the dog has a soul, this observation alone would be sufficient to convince us of the fact ; we see that it is soul-power which moves the creature.

Now, its reverence desires also to make itself manifest ; the dog is eager to show the same in making of itself the willing servant.   It watches the effect of its endeavors and is delighted at its master's kind approval.   This gives evidence of the drift of the creature's ambition.   This feeling acts upon its conscientiousness, and thereby we are shown how keenly the dog is appreciative of the harmony existing between itself and its master.   And it is the power of this feeling, which, on occasions, prompts the animal to raise its benevolence even to the degree of self-sacrifice. Altogether, it appears that the exercise of these higher faculties, under favorable conditions, produces in the soul of the dog a degree of pleasurable feeling far above that attained by many a human being.   As a result, we find this dog to be a light-hearted creature, almost always ready for exchange of pleasantries with its fellows and superiors.   A like condition is noticeable in various other highly developed species, for instance, in the horse.

But now we have to consider this wealth of feeling-power also as it appears when ungratified. Let the dog lose its home and playmates ; deprive it of their good will, and see how it suffers! Let it be taken from its master, and observe what painful efforts it makes to find him again. Let its master die; and the faithful dog sits by the grave and, wailing, starves until it also dies! Its grief makes it oblivious of all else, and thus indicates to what a high degree the creature has been happy. Why should noble sentiment meet with such an end?

In looking about in the world of animals and taking note of the variety of fates to which the individual creatures are subject, we find the conditions there to be distributed as promiscuously as they are on the plane below, only in greater variety and contrast; while the ultimate attainment of every animal, as well as that of every plant, appears to be nothing beyond annihilation. We will, then, leave the animal plane and look into the fate of the individual in our own sphere, the human.

CHAPTER XIII.

VARIETY OF FATES AND CHARACTERS ON THE HUMAN PLANE.

OUR purpose does not require that we travel about among all the races of the Earth; for, in our own civilized community are to be found all the various kinds of fate, all the contrasts between the different feelings which the great Spirit ever demonstrates in the form of human life.

In this higher world of motion we find as many different fates as there are souls to live through them. Although the human souls are all combinations of the animal characteristics, we find, nevertheless, also on our plane individual representations of each of the propensities in separate. We find one person given up almost entirely to the impulse of acquisition; he is the personification of greed. Another is dominated altogether by the propensity to destroy; a third, by some other animal desire, and so forth; each propensity is almost the exclusive owner of a number of lives; and these being human souls, its manifestation through them is, of course, vastly more pronounced than it could be on the lower plane. So, also, is the character of the consequent fate more clearly defined with respect to details. These lives are caused chiefly by the aggravating influences which sometimes gather in superior strength about a certain individual and his family, promoting the activity of the lower faculties, while at the same time impeding the development of the higher. They are the boundary-marks of human life in the direction of darkness.

Likewise do we find the higher traits each represented in certain souls in such prominent degree as to be practically the master of the individual. Thus, we know of instances where the desire for friendship is so pronounced that the death of the one friend means also the death of the other. Love of home, desire for praise, the higher moral sentiments, as, for instance, veneration, benevolence, conscientiousness, etc., are each almost the sole owner of a number of persons. In a third direction, we meet with those in whom the all-powerful voice is given to the separate faculties of the intellect: One will sacrifice all his feelings to his love of art; another lives only for the pursuit of some branch of science. Each of these human souls, in its singleness of purpose, goes

out into the world of life to establish with all the
powers at its command the boundary-mark, or
outside limit, of a single faculty.   Thus does the
Spirit extend in all directions the conscious life of
the community as a whole ; and this remains ever
intact, because each phase of life is always to be
found somewhere represented by some one or
more individuals.

The contemplation of these various feelings in
their extremes aids us in forming the true esti-
mate of their relative values.   We have observed
their effect upon the animals and know it also
from personal experience.   We find that the faculties exert the same kind of influence on our
plane that characterizes them on the lower; the
feelings which they give rise to are merely intensi-
fied : First, our body, being more refined, enjoys
a higher degree of pleasurable feeling; but it is
also more easily hurt and possesses greater capacity for suffering.   The nerves which watch over
the safety of the human body are necessarily
more alive to report whatever disturbance may
come to any part.   Thus our body must pay for
the refinement of its pleasurable feelings with an
increased susceptibility to pain.   Then, the propensities pertaining to the bodily functions cause
in the one direction a higher degree of enjoy-

ment; in the other, greater misery. For, that which they seek to gratify is not the body of a simple animal soul, but that of a human. Likewise the social and all the other higher and lower desires in the interest of the self must cause increased intensity of feeling in both directions; for they are human; they pertain to the human world and to all that comes forth therein.

Now, we have long ago observed that the world of creatures is an inseparable part of the world of substance. This, we have seen, is created for the particular purpose of demonstrating changes in relationships. All creatures dependent upon the world of substance are compelled to share its destiny: that of an everlasting state of warfare, in which they all must find their place and also their destruction. All things in this world of strife that are dear to us, are liable at any moment to be taken from us, — and the pleasure of possession turns into the pain of loss. All earthly bonds of soul and body are destined at some time to be cut in two; and thus, in looking about at all the human lives which people our Earth, we become aware that in their midst are at every moment represented all the various kinds of feeling, from the highest happiness of which man is capable down to his deepest misery. We see that

the Spirit demonstrates its contrasts of life as
things of simultaneous existence.   Now we ask,
"How are these conditions of the soul divided
among the individuals?"   A single glance shows
us that there is as great a variety of contrast prevailing between the fates of the entire lives as
there is between the contents of the moments.
Not alone are the powers of life, or feeling,
unequally distributed, but likewise the opportunities for their gratification : One has all the powers
of feeling which happiness requires, but cannot
enjoy for want of the proper chance ; another is
favored with opportunities, but lacks the powers
of feeling ; a third is happy in the possession of
both ; a fourth, again, is not blessed with either,
and his life passes away as one long, gloomy
shadow.   Then we see how the lives differ in
respect to their duration.

Man naturally pins his happiness to the gratification of his desires, of whichever kind these may
be ; and when either his body or soul is, through
adverse influences, disturbed in the activity peculiar to his nature, he finds himself in pain.   Is
the happy or unhappy fate of man his own making, or does it depend on influences beyond his
power?   On close observation we find that every
life is shaped at the same time from within and

without. Each person simultaneously moves and is moved. Each one presses onward in the direction of his individual preference, and each one's course must likewise suffer constant alteration by the motions of the World surrounding. Fortune, the all-powerful creature, which moves along through the well-connected chain of the World's events, thus leads one person through a life of pleasure to a peaceful death, and another through the very opposite to end in agony.

Now we ask, "Do these various fates come to the respective individuals deservedly?" A comparison between the fates and the characters which experience the same makes it apparent to us that the former are never precisely in accord with the latter; indeed, the two appear to us as being often widely inconsistent with each other. In our estimation of the proper course of justice, the person who is the most active in the interest of his fellow-beings should be the one most kindly treated; while the one who proceeds in the opposite direction should in every instance meet disaster. And yet, how many a noble act brings misery upon the doer, and how often does a selfish deed return to whence it came, apparently not in the form of punishment, but rich reward! So may a man through sheer wickedness acquire fortune and a powerful position, be an oppressor of the poor, squander the substance which he steals from others, in the gratification of his animal desires, — and yet be smiled upon by Fortune and an extensive circle of applauding friends. His is but the undeveloped animal-soul having at its command a human body and a human intellect. His conscience is but small, and therefore cannot trouble him in just proportion to the degree in which he troubles others. His life may even find a painless end. So, on the other hand, may one whose very virtues hinder him from rising in the World, who, moreover, sacrifices the little that he has to the good of others, — be condemned to suffer a life of misery and persecution, and to ultimately end in poverty and pain, forsaken by the world of fellow-beings even long before he is allowed to die. Between these two extremes of worldly fortune we find distributed the multitude of contrasts in reward and punishment for good and evil: As the Sun shines equally upon the just and the unjust, so may fall upon them both the shadow of misfortune. Moreover, we cannot close our eyes to the discovery, that, even if the individuals were able to insure the acquisition of the worldly favors through nobility of conduct, these goods would still remain beyond the reach of many; for, the chances of developing the necessary character are unevenly divided. Let us consider this fact for a moment.

We have seen how the Spirit evolves the faculties of man by means of the three principles: Space, Substance, and Motion. These three are as indispensable on one plane of existence as they are on the other; neither of them can come forth anywhere without the other two being present also. Character is the outcome of the relations existing between the various faculties. It is thus the product of the three principles. Viewing it in the sense of being an object under consideration, we may here regard it as constituting the substance; it follows that the appearance and development of this object require motion, exercise, as well as a space, a sphere, in which to move. Have all characters a like supply of these three essentials? Of the various kinds of occupation in the community each requires a superior exercise of a certain set of faculties to a corresponding neglect of the others. While, for instance, the occupation of the business man tends to increase the activity in the faculties of acquisitiveness and secretiveness in preference to those of veneration and spirituality, the vocation of the preacher is calculated for an effect directly

the reverse.   The one occupation is as necessary
to the welfare of the community as the other;
but each brings the soul into a different sphere of
action, and the characters which are to move in
this sphere and through their exercise to develop,
must necessarily adapt themselves to the limits
by which they find themselves surrounded.   We
may find, here and there, persons that seem to be
originally designed to fill with a beneficial influence a sphere of wide proportions, through adverse
circumstances remain confined within a world of
action so small and far beneath their station, that,
in sheer despair over their imprisonment, they let
go their hold upon their aspirations, and, for the
time being, sink back into the depths of vice and
misery : the lesser sphere has obdurately hindered
the activity of the higher powers, while encouraging that of the lower.   Again, there are souls
of smaller powers of expansion, which, through
outer influences, drift into a higher sphere than
they seem to be intended for, and by the power
of its influence become impelled, even against
their individual inclination, toward reaching out
beyond their personality, so that eventually they
may attain a comparatively elevated state of being :
these have received more motion and a larger
sphere in which to move, and thus assume an

appearance of being superior in their nature to the former, less favored persons.

Such are the extremes of fortune as regarding the conditions offered for development of character. Human life appears to us a perpetual moving about of differently developed beings through one another's places. Those of the greatest movability are the ones most favored with chances for development, inasmuch as they pass through the greatest variety of spheres of action. But, like the trees which crowd each other in the forest, not one is in any sphere permitted an unfoldment perfectly symmetrical in all directions; for the conditions are never thus encouraging. Now, we might say, " Unfavorable influences may be overcome through a superior exercise of will." However, as we know, will-power is, like all the other constituents of character, a faculty the relative strength of which is determined within the individual from the beginning of his life. No two characters are endowed with an equal share of this force; its apparent superabundance in one person is offset by a corresponding deficiency in another; and, of course, each can exercise that only which he has. The power of will is to grow through the medium of its exercise; but in the course of its development we see it often succumb to forces that are at the moment still superior. Thus we find that the beauty and power of the soul are as much dependent upon the joint action of both the individual and his surroundings, as are the health and strength of the body, and the favors of this World in general. Nothing in this Universe can ever take its course independently. In order that the unfoldment of its principles from the World's foundation upward may continue in the proper order, the Universal Spirit must forever keep the fates of all its creatures closely interwoven, and continue throughout to be the sole directing power over each and all in every smallest detail; or the World would at once disintegrate.

We have already perceived that there is no power but that of the Universal Spirit, and that nothing can find existence in this Universe which is not called for by the voice of necessity. We know that this call is a continuous one, and that there is none other possible which could make itself perceptible in opposition to it. This demand for strict consistency between that which is and that which is to be is, in other words, the call for *Justice*. We may feel assured that the Spirit responds to each such call, because the Spirit itself is the source of each, and because this is

the only way in which the World can remain
intact. However much the human sense may
shrink from acknowledging the fact : it still remains the truth that the evil as well as the good,
the misery as well as the happiness, come forth
into the World because necessity demands them
all. For the same reason is the fate of individuals not consistent with the character of their
life. How could this unequal distribution take
place if the omnipotent Spirit did not will it
thus ? The eye of the personality may not perceive the justice which regulates our fates ; for
Justice, the true and the real, is the life of the
Spirit itself. The human eye sees that part of
its operation merely which becomes visible from
an individual point of view ; and, the personal
powers of perception being limited in all directions and not evenly proportioned amongst one
another, the little which they do reflect must ever
appear more or less vague and distorted. Therefore we know, that reality is always different
from its appearance to the individual. And thus
we find that Justice, this system of reward and
punishment, has, in truth, not that nature which
the limited human mind attributes to it. The
more the soul expands beyond the sphere of its
own personality, the more clearly does it perceive

that he who seeks Justice in its appearances merely, will never find it.   Justice is greater than reward and punishment ; it is of a higher nature ; and, therefore, he who would acquire a true conception of it, must first rise out of the sphere of the personality.   We, who are still creatures of the Earth, each confined within his own limited sphere, struggling for existence, constantly subject to alternate happiness and misery, pursuing the one and shrinking from the other, — we will make the attempt to rise out for the moment and see what views we can obtain of the secret nature of this Divine Justice which shapes our destinies, and upon the right conception of which depends our ultimate well-being.

CHAPTER XIV.

THE REASON FOR OUR SUFFERINGS; OUR RELATION TO THE EVIL.

LET us, then, begin with the question, "Why does the all-powerful, the all-wise, and harmonious Spirit cause its creatures to suffer?" — When we sum up the observations that we have so far made, we shall find that the answer to this question is practically already contained within them: We have seen that the World with all its creatures is the personality, the medium, through which the Spirit feels its existence. Each creature demonstrates one phase of the Spirit's life, or power of feeling. Now, when we look once more into the nature of the fundamental principles, we are reminded that each of them is but a demonstration of relationship between parts, a manifestation of *contrast*. That which cannot be compared with something else, is impossible of existence. This idea of contrast is therefore the structure upon which the World is built. We have seen that in its ideas of Space, Substance, and Motion the Spirit establishes contrast primarily with respect to extent. Following the course of their unfoldment, we have observed how the Spirit further causes them to make their relationships manifold: the more contrasts, the more existence. Thus we perceive, first, the simple contrast between Space and Substance: an object needs its volume of Space in which to exist. Then we see how light is offset by darkness: light is vibration, motion of substance; the substance requires a space in which to move, to vibrate, and this motion cannot become apparent unless there simultaneously appears a state of calm, or another kind of motion — as a contrast. Thus, light needs for its existence a space of darkness, and we must know the darkness before we can become conscious of the nature of light. In like manner do the vibrations of life fill out the abyss of death. Each of these exists only through the contrast between itself and its opposite; and the soul which is to reflect the one, must necessarily have also received into itself the likeness of the other.

We understand that life is the most perfect harmony of vibration. Death means the most complete discord, a condition in which the general counteraction is so perfect that out of this chaos nothing whatever can come forth and make itself by any means perceptible. Harmony is felt by us as happiness; discord, as misery. These two fill out our entire life; they are the world of contrasts perceived through our power of feeling. The more strongly these are reflected within us, the more do we feel, or live; and it is quite obvious, that, if either of the two were missing in our experience, the other would be imperceptible, too, and therefore would not exist to us : the soul must have personally felt the pain before it can become aware of the nature of the opposite, pleasure. For instance, it would be impossible for us, if we had never had any bodily discomfort, to consciously enjoy a state of bodily well-being. Our knowledge of pain could, in that case, be merely an intellectual one. Not even could our imagination then create for us a picture which our feelings could recognize. As the power of feeling lies neither in the intellect, nor in the imaginative faculties, we should be unable to contrast any picture of pain that we might see with our condition of health, so far as feeling is concerned : No suffering, — no enjoyment. This contrast between pain and pleasure is as necessary for the enjoyment of the higher feelings as it is for that of the lower. How clearly is this shown, for instance, with respect to home and

friends : who ever appreciates these so keenly as
the one who has been without them for a while?
All gratifications of the soul are subject to the
same law of contrast, — even the moral ; for each
of them is an experience of a certain harmony in
the feelings succeeding its opposite, the discordant state of feelings ungratified ; and this contrast
between the feelings of the individual is the purpose for which the changeful character of our
existence is maintained, — even that of our moral
existence.

Here we are reminded of the fact that the
greater part of human suffering arises from what
we call " evil thoughts and deeds," themselves to
us the greatest of all discords.   Let us now seek
to discover the true relation in which the world
of humanity stands to these.

To begin with : What constitutes the evil character?   In its most pronounced form it is the
conscious desire to cause discord for its own sake ;
in other words, the willful assertion of self in
opposition to the character of the Universal
Spirit.   We see that it arises from the selfish
propensities.   Do we find it, then, in the animal-
world?   No ; for the animals are too little conscious of the nature of the World for them
ever to perceive the same as being an object

for willful opposition.   The lion, for instance, is
not morally responsible for the murders which he
commits; he has no other motive than preservation of self, and his propensities must act accordingly; he knows nothing of the higher Law.
Even the cat which destroys a mouse without
devouring the same is not considered as having
done anything which does not accord with the law
of its life.   Cat and mouse are placed in their
relation to each other by the law of the Spirit, so
that the mice may be prevented from killing too
many of the smaller animals.   The cat, in turn,
is hindered by others from doing away with too
many mice.   The Spirit preserves the animal-
world in proper equilibrium by way of directing
the various species to exercise their destructiveness upon one another.   The cruelty of the cat
toward the mouse is nothing worse than the
animal's gloating over the capture of its enemy.
Animals cannot become truly conscious of the
pain which they inflict, and are therefore not to
be considered as being what we call "evil."

We must look for the evil character on our own
plane: When a human soul is active enough to
discern the difference between harmony and discord in others, and, notwithstanding, permits its
animal propensities to predominate over its higher

faculties, the character of that soul may be considered as being consciously bad. The higher faculties have, in such a case, either not yet developed, or their development has, through a train of adverse circumstances, suffered a temporary retrogression. The lower impulses are without their proper guide. Being in the human body, their clamor for gratification is so much the more terrible; and, by the help of the intellect, the discord which they create within the soul acquires the character of system. The finer voice, which would cause the individual to recognize his true relationship toward his fellow-creatures and to rightly appreciate the value of harmony, remains for the time imperceptible.

However, even the worst of characters is not allowed to remain in its original condition; what is lacking in proper guidance within, is supplied by forces coming from without. It is the Law that every force must meet its opposition: as the Spirit preserves the equilibrium on the lower plane by setting the propensities of each creature against those of the others; so does it, in the same manner, maintain the proper balance on the plane of human life by causing the faculties of each individual to be responded to by those of the whole community. Every vibration must radiate as such into the surroundings; and, as the sound which strikes the wall must always come back to its source truly echoed, so is also each act destined to be felt, sooner or later, by the individual from whom it went forth, either agreeably or painfully, according to the motive which prompted it. Thus, an evil deed is responded to on the human plane in the nature of punishment; the painful effect upon the perpetrator is calculated to arouse his undeveloped or dormant conscience, so that he may cease imagining that disturbances can ultimately bring him any pleasure.

Where the individual conscience is so far awakened that evil is no more regarded as the end, but merely as the means to an end, we perceive the character of the ordinary animal-soul, which is controlled by the desire for preservation of self at any cost. In the human this desire is stronger and more manifold, because his wants are greater and more numerous; and the consequences of the gratification of this desire at the expense of fellow-creatures are therefore also more severe. He meets with greater opposition, and his suffering is more intense. Thus his consciousness is led to gradually develop into the power to perceive *why* the rights of others are to be respected, so that this higher sense may then guide him toward finding the *way* in which it should be done. Accordingly, he learns to give attention to the promptings of the higher self, and his moral faculties receive their due exercise and consequent development. Thus takes place within each individual a gradual evolution from moral discord toward moral harmony.

Now, however, we are reminded of the fact that very often the evil is apparently not responded to in the form of punishment. On careful observation we find that this, too, has its well-defined reason : When we consider how morally undeveloped the human soul is, we also become aware of its comparative weakness. If the full force of Justice were to come upon it suddenly, the soul would not be able to pay its dues; it would be bankrupt, that is, the soul has as yet not done so much of that which is selfless as it has of the opposite ; it has not given so much as it has taken. Nor has it evolved a power which would enable it to cover the deficiency by any immediate act, if such an one were suddenly demanded. If the deeds which the soul, prompted by the impulse of self-preservation, performs through the medium of its body, were each time immediately followed by their just consequences upon the latter, the soul would not get a chance to maintain a body at all, and would therefore become an impossibility. That which impels the soul to live is, if we will take a general view of the subject, nothing else than the desire for gratification. According to how far the soul has evolved, will its desires be low or high. An individual of a low, undeveloped character cannot yet perceive any pleasure in that which is moral; therefore he cannot yet be moved to direct his energies toward procuring the enjoyments of the higher kind. Still, his soul wants to be gratified, or it would be without the necessary impulse to exist. Therefore, not yet being fit for the true kind of gratification, it is permitted at intervals to enjoy the apparent; the payment for the same being temporarily suspended. Thus is preserved the strength and the impulse of the undeveloped soul to remain in existence.

Meanwhile, the individual's gradually awakening conscience succeeds in making its voice more and more plainly perceptible in the very midst of his apparent pleasures, discouraging their repetition through the painful feelings which it causes within him; and thus leading him gradually toward a condition where the higher faculties have sufficiently evolved to enable him to perceive that he has contracted a debt : where he at last shall feel impelled to begin its payment according to the Spirit's Law; placing his personality in the service of his creditor, the Universal Spirit. Thus we see how evolution is possible only through an enforced *compromise* among all creatures.

In looking about among the various characters, we have observed that they all differ from one another in degree of development; and this observation leads us to a clear understanding of the relation in which the evil stands to the good with respect to purpose : We see that the evil character does not meet with opposition from merely the lower faculties of the community, but likewise from the higher. While the former compel the individual to moral progress by way of meeting like with like, the latter exercise upon him the power of persuasion : the beings of higher development meet the evil with good ; they exert upon the transgressor their power for good by sending his vibrations of discord back to him in the form of harmony, and thus giving him an opportunity for better comparison between the two. He thus becomes acquainted with the nature of the higher character by personal inner contact, learns to sense through his own feelings the superiority of the gratifications enjoyed by a character that emanates a harmony so powerful, and, as is quite natural, becomes encouraged to an effort of substituting these for his own. The example is before him; and, as we know, the gentle power of persuasion contained in its placid demonstration of imperturbable serenity and kindness proves in the end to be the stronger force. And this is the feature in which we may discover the reason why the good are so often placed in contact with the various kinds of evil influence: We have seen how all things come forth through exercise alone, and how character is one of these. Character demands for its elevation a frequent active demonstration in the direction of goodness. This exercise, however, always requires that the performer have an object upon which to act; and this must be an object of resistance, something to cause a more or less painful effort. We may compare this exercise of the soul to that of our arm while lifting weights: like this, the soul must, in order to evolve its power of ascent, constantly practise upon something that tends to bear it down; and this object of resistance, in this case, consists in the evil influence. When the exercise of the arm causes a certain feeling of soreness, we consider this an indication that we are adding somewhat to our strength of muscle. The absence of this feeling proves that there has been comparatively little effort, and consequently only little progress. This applies with equal force to the soul. For instance, when a suggestion comes to us, calculated to arouse our self-interest, which then clamors for gratification at the expense of our neighbor, we naturally, for the time being, suffer the pains of discord. We call our higher faculties to increased activity. When, finally, these have prevailed and once more peace is restored within, then we feel that through this exercise we have gained in moral power, in force of elevation ; we have benefited by the evil suggestion. In the same way, when we have been injured by an erring fellow-man, and, instead of meeting like with like, we exert ourselves in the work of kindly lifting him out of the misery of his fault, the effort of showing him that which we perceive as being right and good, causes these perceptions to become so much the more clearly apparent to ourselves. Better perception of harmony means stronger love of harmony, and makes clear the way to its attainment. The forces required for our progress have been increased through the exercise which they were compelled to undergo ; thus we have benefited by the evil deed.

We may, then, look upon all the evil, which is the cause of so much of the misery through which we are obliged to pass, as being in this World for the express purpose of making possible the evolution of the good. In every respect the good and the evil exist for one another, just like any other pair of opposites that we may think of. The good, too, can become perceptible through its contrast only with the opposite, the evil.

This principle, contrast, contains one more feature to be considered; and this is a most important one: We find that the feelings of pain and pleasure do not depend merely upon the extent of contrasts experienced, but also upon the manner in which these experiences of contrasts follow one another. When we have for some time continued in one certain condition, the feeling attendant upon the same gradually loses its power to impress. The recollection of its contrast with a former state fades away from us. A new condition, a new experience of contrast, — and our power of feeling is again aroused to higher activity. Thus our pain or pleasure increases or diminishes according to the amount of time which elapses while we move from one condition into another. We will consider, for instance, the feelings of the body in health and

in sickness: A man has for years been in good
health. He has gradually become so accustomed
to this that he has nearly lost the recollection of
ever having been in any other condition; therefore he is now likewise almost unconscious of his
pleasurable state of health. Suddenly, however,
he becomes ill. Now his feelings are aroused.
He becomes painfully aware of a growing contrast
between his present condition and the former.
After a while, when the picture of sickness has
once more become strongly impressed upon his
feelings, he begins to recover. By degrees his
body returns into its usual harmonious condition
and regains its former strength. He perceives
how each day the contrast between misery and
well-being widens in his favor; and it is this
motion in which he is engaged as he passes from
degree to degree, that must force his powers of
feeling to their close attention. These are compelled to watch the course of improvement taking
place in the body with the same vigor that they
evinced during the process of its deterioration;
at no other times can they be so active. And
thus, the same law, which, during the time of his
getting sick, caused him to experience the most
acute form of misery, must now, during his progress in the opposite direction, grant him the high-

est degree of pleasure: he finds that *getting* well is more pleasurable than *being* well. This law applies not alone to the conditions of the body, but likewise to those of the soul. In every instance the highest potency of feeling has its being in the perception of the change itself.

Through causing our feelings thus to alternately increase and diminish their activity, ever fluctuating between discord and harmony, work and rest, the Spirit preserves and increases their power. In the fact that the most painful feeling in the soul arises from a perception of moral retrogression, while the most pleasurable comes forth as a consequence of moral progress, we have a conclusive evidence that the Spirit preserves the life of the soul for no other purpose than for the demonstration of progress in the direction of well-being through moral evolution. Through the law of contrast we are shown the right direction by the pain that our moral sense encounters in the opposite. In all things we are constrained to suffer before we can enjoy.

At this point, however, we are reminded of the observations that we made before, and now there forces itself upon our mind that great question: "If progress in the direction of well-being is our destiny, why are, nevertheless, so many creatures doomed to undergo more misery than happiness, and why do so many lives end in suffering?" Let us try to find an explanation.

CHAPTER XV.

WE have convinced ourselves that the Spirit's
final object is the evolution of feeling through the
medium of variety of experience, demonstration
of contrast. Now, however, we are not to understand, that, as a creature's unhappy moments are
the necessary background to its happy ones; so
a whole life of misery should be called forth to
serve as offset merely to another life consisting of
pleasure. For, as we know, the Spirit demonstrates the power of feeling, or life, alone through
the medium of its individual creatures; in other
words, feeling cannot exist independently of the
created being. The Spirit radiates its life into
the various souls as the Sun sends his vibrations
into the bodies, and there only can the feeling be
generated. Thus we see that a body which combines within itself the sensations of all creatures
at once, does not exist.

We have observed, while following the course
of evolution from the very first principles upward,

that the Spirit in its wholeness is alike present within each of its creatures. We, of course, are not able to detect the presence of all the faculties in every form of life, but these are, nevertheless, present in the germ in each creature, and only awaiting the opportunities required for their development. Likewise is the Spirit's character of progressiveness expressed in every life, and this character remains ever the same. The one Spirit being equally present in all its creatures, and at the same time directing their fates in common, it is quite impossible that any one of these should ultimately receive better consideration than the rest. And such a thing as blind chance is out of the question altogether; for the various fates are so closely interwoven with one another, that no room is left for anything which is not called forth by a demand of necessity. There certainly is no necessity for an unequal distribution of good throughout Eternity. How could the all-wise and all-powerful Spirit, which maintains the Universe by its will, the character of which is harmony, deliberately create anything for the purpose of final discord? This would prove that the Spirit were divided against itself; for the proceeding would be an injustice such as even the human being of ordinary development would not commit.

And how could the Creator, who at all times maintains his power over his creations, and whose wisdom must ever remain beyond the comprehension of any individual soul, wish to be less just to any of his creatures than they would be to one another? The existence and continuance of the World proves that harmony is the ruling power; if it were not, there would be no possibility of any thing to make itself perceptible above the perfect discord, the chaos, the "no-thing." When the Spirit succeeds in evolving one of its souls into a condition of happiness, it certainly has the power to do the same by all the others; for it is equally present in all. Where in any one the discord ultimately acquired the ascendancy over the harmony, there the Spirit would have suffered a final loss; it would have proven itself weak. Is such an event to be thought possible for only a moment? Every line of life-experiences must upon closer observation show that the soul which goes through them is stronger at the end than it was at the beginning; for the individual goes through a series of *exercises*. Even though a soul be apparently unsuccessful, miserable, and finally vanish from the scene as a defeated warrior, — the energy with which it fights its last battle is superior to that with which it came to Earth. Its

qualities in general have improved in exact proportion with the amount and greatness of hardships overcome.   In the course of its troubled
career some of the powers of the soul may apparently vanish, that is, they may disappear from *our*
view. · But, can a power once possessed by the
soul ever be lost?   When a force has disappeared,
there still remains the possibility of proving that
this force has merely for the time being become
latent through the influence of some other force,
or else, that its medium is no longer suitable for
its use.

Let us picture to ourselves the course of one
of these lives that end in defeat : We will suppose it to be that of a man ending as a slave to
the lower appetites.   When he first comes to
Earth, we see him as a child, in appearance very
much resembling all other children.   The little
one is not yet quite conscious of its own being ;
it is still free from care.   This condition expresses
itself in the features, and the distinguishing marks
of the individuality are thus to a great extent still
hidden from view.   The body is yet small and
weak, and the soul within cannot fully express
itself, until it has put this little body through
a course of development.   The brain, however,
already contains the required organs, and, upon

close observation, it may be noticed that its proportions are, from the very start, as different from
those of all other brains as the soul within differs
from all other souls. This fact now begins to
make itself more and more manifest in the child's
features and ways in general. As yet, however,
no one discovers any indication of the great evil
which is lurking within, awaiting its opportunity
to develop. The evil remains still hidden in the
bud; it has not yet the means with which to show
itself. Eventually, the child evolves into man-
hood, and the man is at liberty to enter as a
responsible factor the world of activity and temp-
tations. Now all the qualities of his soul have
an equal chance to come forth and to express
themselves. Until now, his life has been such as
to encourage the action chiefly of the higher faculties. The training which he received did not
permit any gratification of the lower self beyond
the degree of moderation. While the higher self
was being cultivated, his animal faculties were
counteracted, hindered from their full expression;
they have to that degree remained *latent*, and
their further fate now depends upon his own free
judgment. We will suppose that they were originally more powerfully represented than their
opposites. The result is that they will now grad-

ually come forth and make their nature felt with superior energy and tenacity; they clamor for individual gratification. The training received by the higher faculties has not been quite sufficient to raise these into such superiority over the propensities that they might now keep these latter in subjection and press them into service on the higher plane. The man's powerful impulse toward preservation of self thus becomes more and more confined to the interests of the body. He is led to pay superior attention to that which is attainable on the material plane. He does not now desire to merely preserve the body, but to preserve it *well*. This means, he is anxious that its sensations should be as pleasurable as possible. Thus he feels attracted toward a life of material enjoyment, and, as a consequence, enters the society of those similarly inclined. All this while, his moral faculties are just as active as they would have been under other circumstances, and even more so; for they, in their comparative weakness, yet perceiving the danger of the course pursued, are forced to be the more energetic, the greater the opposing power. There takes place many an inward battle, many a strong remonstrance against the undue animal indulgence; and each such exercise of the higher faculties must

necessarily increase their power.   Meantime, however, also the lower must grow, from the same
cause.   Moreover, through the excessive demands
which the appetites make upon the body, constantly exposing the same to all kinds of destructive influences, this becomes so exhausted that it
gradually deteriorates in the quality of its texture.
The brain loses its power to perform the fine
vibrations required for bringing thought and sentiment into the sphere of personal consciousness,
and thus the higher faculties of the soul are gradually deprived of the service of their organs in
this body.   And this is the direct cause of their
defeat in this man's life : For want of a proper
medium through which to express themselves,
they are finally forced to leave the body in the
sole possession of the animal propensities, taking
with them, of course, the power of judgment
concerning the body itself.   In consequence, this
latter then soon ceases to be serviceable even to
the lower faculties, and must be abandoned by
these also.   In the first part of this man's life
the propensities were latent ; in the latter part,
the higher faculties ; and with this condition came
the end.   The soul has suffered a moral defeat.
But are we justified in supposing this to be a final
one ?   We have seen nothing further than the

reason why the higher faculties were forced to abandon their body before this itself disintegrated.

We are, moreover, aware that destruction is the ultimate destiny of all bodies, irrespective of the height of development attained by the soul within. But the fact that *we* no longer see the power which animated a body, is not a proof that this power has deteriorated or ceased to exist.

We know that Justice demands the like ultimate destiny for all souls, but we see no two individuals end their career at the same point. The Spirit, which maintains the Universe intact throughout the ages, certainly has the power of evolving from the discord the highest form of harmony in all souls alike; it need not restrict itself to leading them through only such a line of experiences as is contained in one short Earth life. Moreover, when we observe the two extremes, the happy form of life and the unhappy one, we stand before the question, "How did those who live either of these two acquire the power of feeling necessary for the conscious perception of their condition?" As we have seen, the law of contrast requires, that, in order to experience with the feelings the one condition, one must have previously had a personal experience of the other; in order to know the taste of a thing, we must have tasted the same ourselves. One might suggest that the soul inherits this knowledge of foreign experiences in the form of intuition; and it cannot be denied, that, as the body inherits certain characteristic qualities, so the soul may receive from the parents a certain share of intuitive knowledge. However, when we consider that at some time or other every family must die out, that through the great catastrophes, such as, for instance, cataclysms, which occur from time to time and revolutionize the conditions on the surface of the planet, whole races of beings in a still undeveloped state are suddenly wiped out of existence, we find that the law of heredity is surely not the only medium of evolution. This fact becomes most clearly apparent to us when we consider the character of the great and good souls which now and then grace the Earth with their presence in human form. These are in power of thought and feeling so far superior to the whole race in which they are born, that, with respect to them, the laws of heredity can have had little or no influence. Each soul is to evolve its powers through the experiences of its own life.

Therefore, as the soul is destined for the highest evolution, as it is to gather the experiences through which to evolve, not through the medium of the law of heredity, but by its efforts as an individual, and as these necessary experiences cannot possibly all be gained in one Earth-life, — there is only one way in which the soul may accomplish its purpose : the soul must preserve its individuality entirely independent of the body, so that when its life in one body has come to an end, it may enter another, and thus forever freely move from life to life. Why should this not be the case? When the soul has the power to form and manipulate one body, why should it not be able to repeat the process? Let us see what proofs we can find that the soul is thus immortal.

CHAPTER XVI.

THE SOUL'S IMMORTALITY AND NECESSITY FOR REAPPEARANCE ON EARTH.

WE will begin by reviewing what we have learned of the World's character in respect to immortality in general: We have seen that the vibrations of the Spirit retain their individuality throughout all their combinations with one another. Not an atom of that which is perceptible to us can ever vanish from existence. The smallest particle of dust floating in the air is as important a part in the fabric of the Universe as the greatest heavenly body, and, like this, exerts its influence throughout the World. Were it possible to annihilate even so small an object as this speck of dust, the vacancy produced would result in the collapse of the Universe so surely as the removal of a wheel connected with the spring of a clock would cause the stand-still of the works. For the atom represents a vibration, a power of revolution, designed to fit closely into the great chain of the World's activity. Likewise is each life-

.

vibration coming from the Sun an immortal power. We see that its force may lie latent for ages ; but it has not vanished from existence; it will reappear the moment in which the conditions set it free to act.   For instance : the rays of the Sun combine with the elements to form a forest of trees.   In the course of time these turn into coal. The power of these life-vibrations has now become latent.   For ages this bed of coal lies hidden in the bosom of the Earth, until it is found.   Man is the medium through which this latent force is to regain its liberty; the coal is placed in a furnace and ignited.   A part of the substance turns into smoke and ashes, and eventually returns to the Earth once more to unite with the soil. Another part, however, in the form of heat-vibrations, enters the water in a boiler.   The original Sun-rays are now active in the steam. This is concentrated so as to act in one particular direction, its force entering the piston-rod of a machine.   The life is now in the latter.   We will suppose that this machine is used in the manufacture of a musical instrument.   This being completed, the power has once more become latent ; it is in the instrument which it helped to make, again awaiting the favorable conditions that may set it free.   Now the musician comes and, with

him, the necessary conditions.   As he calls forth
the various accords of which the instrument is
capable, the power, in the form of sound-vibration,
enters, together with the life of the melody, the
ear of man, and through his brain touches his
soul.   Here these vibrations of harmonious sound
make themselves perceptible in the character of
what we may call "spiritual warmth."   They
have thus once more turned into life-vibrations;
and the soul, impelled by them to higher activity,
refines its power of thought and feeling, conceiv-
ing ideas which, before, had been beyond its
reach.   The life-vibrations of the Sun are now
contained in these ideas and, together with them,
they eventually enter once more the world of matter in the form of acts.

As we are aware, every act is a motion, a vibration, which must strike some part of the Universe,
whether near or far, and thus cause another
motion; that is, every act, being a transmission of
power, has its certain consequences.   Likewise is
every act in itself a consequence, and we understand that there cannot be an end to consequences
any more than there can be a beginning of causes.
The power which thus skips from place to place,
from object to object, bound fast nowhere, sometimes mysteriously disappearing, then reappearing

with wonderful suddenness and force, being for-ever at once the effect and the cause, proves to be immortal in both directions.   It is an emana-tion of the Spirit itself, and each such motion, however small its vibration may be, eventually alters the Universe in every part.   But, individu-ally, it must ever return from time to time to its original character of life-vibration.

The Sun, as we have seen, is a centralization of such power.   The vibrations which he emanates are immortal.   This being the case, it is self-evident that the nucleus which sends them out, namely, the Sun himself, is equally so.   Suppos-ing the Sun, as a body, were through some catas-trophe suddenly dissolved, his whole store of energy would nevertheless continue in existence; it would simply enter that with which it collided; though changing in appearance, it would retain its character, its mode of activity, and it would know its source as well as it does now.   The same law applies to the energy of the created being: this, too, is a centralization of power, send-ing out its vibrations in the form of thought and deed as independently as the Sun emits his rays. The act being immortal, why not also the actor? While we see the living creature in the midst of its activity, we recognize the existence of its power, or soul, even though we cannot perceive the same otherwise than through the medium of the acts which represent its character. Supposing the creature now lies down and rests : we know that its forces have merely become latent; we expect them to come forth again in due time. Now it sleeps : still we do not doubt their existence ; but where are they now ? We know that they are still connected with that body ; for they manifest themselves from time to time in the form of dreams. The soul is allowing its brain a period of rest, and presently we shall see it reappear within the same and impel the creature to its usual activity. Where does the soul go while its servant sleeps? It may go anywhere and nowhere. While observing the mysterious powers of intuition in plant, animal, and man, we have seen that the soul, as master of the body, is free to travel independently beyond the same through Space and Substance, as well as through Time. The soul is therefore not an object in the material sense. We saw that the life-vibrations which entered that forest and subsequently found their way around through the various elements and through the soul of man, being neither bound, nor lost, anywhere, represented the *condition* merely of that through which

they passed. So does also the soul show itself
as the condition of the creature which represents
it. We see that the soul is also in this respect
like all other forces; and, when we remember
that it, too, is an indispensable part of the Universal energy, and originates from the same
Universal Spirit, we can no longer doubt that the
power which constitutes the soul is indeed an
immortal power.

Now, we have remarked that this force distinguishes itself from the other forces through mani-
festing itself in *organized* form. Our first views of
the nature of life have shown us the superiority of
the organized power over the unorganized. We
have seen how the soul of the plant combines the
various elements according to its own will and
design; the plant is a center of action. We see
there established a *condition* which has the power
of remaining intact in the midst of the restless
elements; the desire for maintaining this organized form of existence is evidenced also in the
fact that this condition constantly reproduces
itself from within the plant. Likewise are both
the power and the desire present in the animal;
while in man this condition evolves into conscious
desire and conscious power. The awakening
creature proves to us that a soul, a condition,

which is defined clearly enough to demonstrate itself as a living being is, by virtue of its individuality, enabled to remain the sole possessor of its body even while the latter sleeps. During dreamless sleep the greater and higher part of the soul, if not active in some other locality, has simply returned into that state of (spiritual) latency in which everything is bound that is not at the time called forth for demonstration by the demands of necessity. The moment in which this call arises, comes forth the soul and once more takes charge of its body as required.

When, for a while, the animation of the body is, so far as we can discern, suspended entirely, the degree of soul-power still maintained within the same must certainly be exceedingly small. And yet, in due time the whole soul may come back and once more take up its wonted habitation.

Now, when the body has been deserted by its soul forever, when we see the creature which a while ago represented a center of vibrating force, disintegrate, we are not to conclude that for this reason the soul-power has dissolved also and returned into the universal energy as a multitude of separate vibrations, just as any other force would do. For, the soul is an *organized* power. Its various faculties have firmly united to manifest themselves as one character, one individual; their powerful desire for preservation of self has become *one and inseparable;* and when the soul has thus for any length of time maintained itself intact in the midst of the world of activity, it is certainly qualified for remaining so in the future, whether it be called to return into the silent bosom of the Spirit, or again to come forth in the form of a creature.

Plant and animal prove their power over Substance unconsciously; man knows that he is of the Law, that is, immortal; for he has the power to consciously perceive Law and, to a degree, even the conscious power of its application. The souls of the lower creatures are immortal through their mere desire to be in existence. Man not only feels the desire to be immortal, but he is also conscious of the power to be so. He clearly perceives that he *is;* he looks into the past, and remembers that he *was;* and conscious of his superiority over the world of matter, he feels that he always *will be:* the same conditions that enabled him to come forth once, will at any time allow him to do so again; and who can doubt the power and the will of the Spirit to repeat these conditions in the future the same as it has done in the past?

Even the soul which leaves the sphere of activity, moved by the desire to thereby end its own existence forever, must eventually return to the scene as an individual being, true to its character. Such a soul has not lost its desire to live; it rejects one certain kind of life merely, namely, that to which its own personality is at the time subjected; and thereby it gives evidence of how pronounced its character as an individual actually is. This soul proves that it has a very pronounced preference for a certain kind of existence, or it would not desire to end its present one. It wants to be gratified according to its own desires; and these, in every instance, arise either directly or indirectly from the personality, thus impelling it with irresistible force to return to that only plane where this personality is permitted to assert itself, namely, the Earth-life.

So must also the soul which passes out in the discord of insanity, come back in order to regain its health. When we take a general view of the causes of insanity, we find that these are either physical or psychological. When the cause lies in the disturbed condition of the brain, the equilibrium is lost through the incapacity of the organ merely to properly express the soul. When the discord appears originally in the soul itself, it is in every case to be traced back to an abnormal activity among the faculties in the direction of some interest pertaining to the self. Though the soul has, for the time being, apparently lost its consciousness of self, it has not by any means dissolved. It still has the power to maintain the life of its body; while the very activity of the soul in asserting the self, however unconscious and discordant these manifestations may be, gives evidence that the soul is only too anxious to preserve its individuality, and that, after leaving its present body, it requires a period of rest merely until it shall be fit to continue the process of its cure in the next.

Finally we must consider the lives and expressions of those individuals whom we recognize as having attained the highest degree of unfoldment possible for man on Earth. These great souls who radiate their beneficial influence into the lives of many generations, these great instructors of mankind, are, as we know, all permeated with the firm conviction that the individuality of the soul can never be lost; and they prove the strength of their conviction, not alone by their arguments, but by their very lives. Living in better harmony with the Spirit's Law than is possible to their less developed fellow-men, they are naturally in position to better understand the Spirit's plans. Thus we must, of course, look up to these more advanced minds as being the most trustworthy authority which we have. We see that the higher form of consciousness which they possess is accompanied by a more perfect love of life. They look upon life as being ours, not for temporary enjoyment merely, but for the purpose of eternal elevation; and they illustrate their teachings by their personal conduct: they use their Earth-lives for no other purpose than that of helping their fellow-men to rise, together with themselves, into that higher form of existence which they, from their exalted position, are enabled to discern. Could these great souls, guided by the Spirit within, so gladly renounce all interest in their own personality, if the Spirit had not in store for them a greater life beyond? There certainly is no stronger proof possible, that the individuality of the soul is immortal, than that which is thus given us by these higher beings in their willingness to sacrifice their own Earth-life in the interest of human evolution. In the gladness of self-sacrifice by which their knowledge is accompanied, we truly sense the boundlessness of the life which emanates from the Spirit's almighty and undying power, — the power of *Love*.

CHAPTER XVII.

CONDITIONS GOVERNING REAPPEARANCE; EVOLU-
TION BEYOND THE HUMAN PLANE.

WE may, then, in all safety, feel assured that
every creature represents a soul as immortal as
the Universe of which it is a part, and that each
soul preserves, not only its character as a well-
defined individuality, but also its power of active
demonstration in the Universal life.   Each is destined to make its reappearance from life to life in
such a body and in such environment as corre-
spond with the nature of its desires.   So long
as these pertain to that which is attainable in
Earth-life, the law of affinity will draw the soul
into an earthly body; for, where could there possibly be a sphere so suitable for seeking the gratification of earthly desires as the one to which the
soul has already become accustomed, namely, the
Earth itself?

The recollections of experiences are, of course,
not to be carried along from one life into another; for each life means a new brain, and each

brain can record the experiences of that personality only to which it belongs.   There is no necessity for a recollection of that which happened to
the soul in a former life : As we have seen, the
sole object of the Spirit is to evolve the power of
feeling, and everything that happens to the personality comes to fulfill this one purpose only.
Each event makes its characteristic impression
upon the soul in the form of either pain or pleasure.   Guided by these feelings, the soul then
evolves its various likes and dislikes, in other
words, its character; and thus the events of each
life are carried into the next, not as cold, dry
recollection of facts, but as power of feeling, *intuition*.   We may find this clearly illustrated in the
manner in which the soul forms and maintains its
physical body.   The knowledge pertaining to the
physical constitution is, originally, purely intuitional; it is so firmly imbedded within us, that, in
order to become conscious of the same, we are
compelled to call to aid our powers of intellectual
perception.   Meantime the soul, which has been
enabled by its instinctive knowledge to form its
body, continues by the same power, unconsciously
to ourselves, to keep it intact.   When the body
has for a while been out of order and then, seem-
ingly without assistance, regains its health, we

say, "Nature has cured herself," and, indeed, the cure is the result of the instinctive work of the soul which governs that body.

When eventually the latter, either suddenly or slowly, becomes unfit for habitation by the soul, in other words, when the body dies, the pain attending this process is simply the remonstrance of the faculties against the impending loss of their wonted medium. Knowing, however, that the powers gained by the soul in one body are to find their due opportunity for demonstration in the next, we understand the spiritual reason why the end-part of life is generally painful. It must be so in obedience to the law of contrast ; the beginning of the young life proves this. See the years of happiness that come to the little child as the soul gradually makes itself at home in its new body. More and more each day the various organs are encouraged, developed, and placed in service to gratify the world of desires that manifests itself within. Each new attainment means a new delight. Could all this happiness be possible if the soul had not first received into itself the reflection of the opposite ?

But now, however, there forces itself upon our notice the fact that each birth, in turn, means another death. Further, we are reminded that there is, indeed, no earthly gratification possible which does not ultimately cause as much pain as it brought pleasure. We find that upon every earthly good there is set a certain price, and that this price must be paid, sooner or later, by the very individual who enjoyed the respective benefit. In the long succession of lives through which the soul must pass while gathering its knowledge, there is surely an abundance of opportunity for the payment of its debts to all its creditors ; and the Universal Spirit, which can preserve the world intact through the exercise of perfect Justice only, in the smallest as well as the greatest matters, makes no discriminations. Thus it will happen again and again that the body loses its strength, its beauty, and its health ; that position and wealth suddenly give place to disgrace and poverty ; that the soul is bereft of its objects of affection, — and all this may come upon us apparently without the slightest trace of justification. And we ask, "Wherefore all these lives, if they are to bring us ever the same kind of alternation between the pleasure and the pain ? must there not, in the course of Eternity, come a time when the human soul grows weary of its constant repetition, — a time when it ceases to take the interest in life required for reappearance ?" The Spirit surely has a just reason

for every one of its institutions, and wisely provides for every need arising in its World.

While studying the life of the animal, we
observed that even the higher faculties are subject as much to misery as to happiness.   We see
that their fate is determined, not alone by themselves, but also by the nature of the objects upon
which they are exercised.   The same rule, of
course, applies also to the faculties of man.   The
worldly favors, fellow-beings, — all things that are
perceptible to a personality, are of the like earthly
nature, perishable ; and whatever higher feelings
are bestowed upon these, are liable to come to
grief the same as the lower impulses.   The pleasure of the higher faculties is higher, more refined ;
but likewise is their misery deeper, more acute.
These manifold discouragements often come to us
apparently undeserved.   We remember that the
various fates are never quite in accord with the
character of the respective individuals.   One reason for this shifted condition between us and the
fates that would be consistent with our present life
has already been found : we saw that this apparently unequal distribution of good and bad is in
each case but a temporary compromise necessi-
tated by the condition of the respective souls.
Now, this constantly unequal distribution surely has

another purpose; we may look upon it as indicating a well-defined intention of the Spirit with regard to our further destiny.

When we consider that all our efforts to alter this changeful condition are in vain; that we are constantly subjected to all manner of disappointment and discouragement; when, further, we see that often it is the best character which meets with the greatest adversity, and that the most advanced souls are altogether indifferent concerning the goods of earth, we become convinced that earthly gratification can not be our final destiny. We have seen that the character which the Spirit expresses in its World, is forever that of progressiveness. A stand-still is impossible; and thus, when a soul has proven that it has outgrown the life in human form and has thus become worthy of rising into a higher sphere, we may feel assured that its desire will be gratified: *there is a form of life above the human.*

The advanced souls prove to us by their lives that this higher existence can be attained by us in no other way than through the evolution of our desires. We cannot rise into a higher sphere until these have severed their connection with the lower. Both our personal experiences and our observations of the lives of others show us, that, without the aid of a certain pressure from without, the evolution of our desire, or character, would be an utter impossibility.   The evolution of Life from plane to plane being the Spirit's sole object in all its manifestations, and the aspirations of the human soul not being quite powerful enough to lift this latter out of its present sphere of gratifications without a pressure from without, it is plain that this needed aid must be provided.   It is clear also that the same can not come to us otherwise than in the form of discouragement with respect to these very gratifications ; and thus we have happily arrived at this comforting truth, namely, that all the discouragements which come to us human-beings are to be looked upon by us solely in this light : they come to wean us from that which is earthly, so that we may become free to turn our attention to that which is in store for us beyond ; they help us discard the gratifications of the lower kind, so that we may prepare ourselves for the higher.

It is obvious that this higher form of existence is not for a community confined to human bodies ; for, desires that have been elevated above the human plane require for their gratification a medium different from the human body.   We see that the physical form of man ever remains subject to accidents, disease and death ; it represents a soul which is still bound by its desires to the world of earthly personalities, and which still requires, for the evolution of its desires into a higher form, a continuous contact on a common basis with a variety of other characters of the human calibre.

We see that the plane of human existence, the earth-plane, regarded as an institution, remains stationary, — a class in the great school of Life, the world of souls each at its appointed time moving in, graduating, and rising out into the one above.

CHAPTER XVIII.

CONCERNING THE HIGHER FORM OF LIFE AND THE WAY IN WHICH IT IS ATTAINED.

LET us now see how far we may comprehend the conditions and nature in general of that higher life which is in store for us. Where are we to look for that higher sphere? It cannot be located on another planet, for each one of these receives its own share of life-vibrations, and must confine itself to the work of evolving the creatures entrusted to it, the same as the Earth is restricted to the evolution of her own. There can be no place on any planet for beings which the same has not itself evolved from the very first stage. The physical conditions to be found on other spheres being different from those on Earth, the bodies of the creatures living there must likewise differ from our own. This is the barrier which prevents us from becoming creatures on any foreign planet: not only are we accustomed to the conditions of our own, but, at the same time, we can get no opportunity for becoming even so much as acquainted with those existing elsewhere. Any adaptation to them is thus out of the question. Therefore other planets have no more power of attraction over our soul than they have over our body. Moreover, there is no call of necessity for such a transfer of existence : there is no reason for supposing that the soul cannot evolve all its faculties and its perception of the Universal harmony just as well in the sphere of the Earth as in that of any of the other planets.

We find that the only way in which we may learn anything concerning the plane above our present one, is by looking into those that lie below, and then following the line of evolution upward so far as we find the same indicated by the lives of those who have risen beyond us.

We have seen how the life comes to the Earth direct from the Sun, and how the Earth then proceeds to form the various unions with these vibrations, bringing forth the plant and the animal. These creatures, we know, belong exclusively to the sphere of Earth. Then we have seen how the union of the various animal-traits forms the soul of man. As these faculties come forth on our planet, it is obvious that the Earth is also the first place where man's soul appeared. It is, of course, impossible for us to discern whether the faculties constituting the human soul have, or have not, been individually and separately evolved in actual life on the lower planes. It does not, however, seem so very improbable, when we bear in mind that all soul-power is to be evolved through exercise in a body. Nor could we prove that each animal-soul had not first to be reflected as a rudimentary idea in the form of vegetation, before it could become well enough defined to demonstrate itself in the world of the more active moving creatures. As all soul-power is immortal and must ever be more or less active, how would the plant and animal-souls otherwise find their opportunity for evolution? We cannot suppose that they are doomed forever to remain on their present plane. This would not be in accord with the Spirit's character of progressiveness, nor would it be just. When, for instance, a dog proves by its individual valor to be an important factor in our lives, perhaps even sacrificing its own body in order to save ours, we could not in justice remain content with the thought that the soul of this friend is doomed to remain forever in its limited sphere, while we, on the contrary, are permitted to rise beyond ours. All forces are constantly employed in the interest of evolution, and, in the economy of the World, none is allowed to remain forever idle or latent.   Thus it seems quite probable that each individual soul must travel through all these planes of existence; that the propensities which move the plants and animals are favored with the same destiny as are those within the human.   The soul which lives in the animal certainly is worthy of uniting with others to inhabit a human body; for, as we have seen, there is to be found clearly represented the facsimile of each within the human soul.   We know, that, in reality, the animal-soul is not beneath us, but within us, the same as the word stands within the sentence.   What should we be, for instance, without the noble dog-soul with its qualities of friendship, faithfulness, and reverence?   On the other hand, has not many a person a greater share of destructiveness than even the tiger? and are not the traits of the pig, the peacock, and the cow, each the master of a host of human souls?   At all events, when we consider how many evidences there are which encourage our conclusion, and that we can find none that proves the same to be wrong, we cannot be far misled when we actually assume that the soul which lives in our body has once inhabited a number of animal-bodies, and that the animals of the present day are destined at some time in the distant future to unite their forces for demonstration on the human plane.

The propensities which constitute the desires pertaining to the preservation of self, determine by the degree of their evolution the sphere of the soul's activity: they confine the plant to the spot and the animal to its species. On the human plane they are in position to alter their mode of activity: instead of restricting themselves to the narrow sphere of the individual, they may now become the powerful propellers of the soul on its way outward into the great beyond as a conscious, individual being; they become what we may call "spiritual energy." The impulse which, on the lower plane, knows only destruction, is elevated on the higher plane into its very opposite, into creative force; the desire for acquisition of material things evolves into love for the attainment of knowledge; the power of reproduction, raised out of the lower plane into the service of the higher faculties, proceeds, true to its nature, to move us and to help us to bring forth "children of the Spirit," ideas. Thus, each finds its appropriate kind of service on all planes of life; but, as we see, the sphere of their activity always remains the Earth.

Let us now follow the course of one of those

souls which have risen out above the human plane. We may certainly learn something of the nature of the higher sphere through studying the character of those who went to live in it. Although we may have never come into personal contact with any of these beings, we are well acquainted with their personality through the history of mankind. We know them by the greatness of the light which their last Earth-life continues to radiate into the lives of the multitude from generation to generation ; and so these men stand before our mind's eye as plainly visible as though we had personally communicated with them from the days of our childhood. To be sure, they are our real personal friends, and as such they enable us step by step to come into a clearer understanding, both of their personality and their world.

To begin, we will observe how one of these souls expresses itself in the features of its body : as we proceed to study the face of the man, the first which preëminently forces itself upon our notice, is the apparent absence of all traces of the animal-soul. Neither here, nor in the form of his head, is there to be found a single line that might suggest an animal-trait ; nor is there any such to be detected in his general bearing. We see at once that this is not the body of the ordinary

animal-man ; we find it to be the exclusive medium
of the higher thought, the spiritual.   The expression of this man shows us that in the course of his
evolution the powers of every one of the animal-
propensities has become completely absorbed by
the higher faculties.   Is the expression a happy
one ?   It is serene ; it calls forth the inference that
the soul within does not derive its pleasures from
the limited sphere of the perishable, the personal,
but has expanded beyond the same.   There is not
a mark of hardness to be found in any of the features ; they are tender, yet strong throughout ; they
show that, personally, he feels himself in harmony,
both with his fate and his Creator.   In short, he
appears what he is : all love for that which brings
true well-being, and compassion for all who are
not yet in possession of it.   No other feeling can
find any room within him beside these two ; he
can hate nothing that the Universe might contain.
However, he is not yet exempt from human suffering ; for, so long as his soul is bound to a human
body, it must feel the influences to which this
body is subjected.   But we see that he has the
power to patiently endure anything that may befall
him.   All these happy qualities are the fruits of
long and persistent personal effort.   This superior
strength and harmony of feeling has come forth

as a result of the course of training which is destined to be experienced by every soul. He has
made himself acquainted with the nature of all the
faculties through personal activity, and has felt
their effect upon himself and others in every
sphere of life through which he has passed. During his career through the various lives he has had
abundant opportunity of perceiving that gratifications at the expense of fellow-beings invariably
turned out in the end to be altogether at his own ;
for he has eventually been forced to pay every such
debt that he had contracted. Then he has gradually become aware that there is, in fact, no earthly
pleasure unaccompanied by its equivalent of pain.
Each such experience has made its impression
within his soul and has remained there in the
form of intuitional knowledge, prompting him in
each successive life to reduce his wants. Having
become thoroughly acquainted with the nature of
personal enjoyment, the soul has begun a search
for sensations of a higher kind: He has reached
out more and more into the realms of spiritual
knowledge. He finds this more gratifying as he
begins to perceive its power of showing the way
to personal independence.

While he was living on the material plane, he
found that the same gratification may be enjoyed

in either of two ways : by taking, or by giving.
He has, already at that period, felt how these
differ in the feeling which they produce.   He has
practised them both, and now, as he rises into the
higher knowledge, he also clearly perceives *why*
the one is preferable to the other.   While he
gratified himself merely, he was feeding the lower,
the selfish propensities; there was then perceptible no voice of approval other than that of the
lower self, the personality.   In being thus nur-
tured, these desires were encouraged to increase ;
each succeeding time they clamored for more,
thus causing a growing painful discord within.
Gratifying them meant the creation of a like discordant condition between himself and the surroundings.   So he found himself subjected to
painful assaults, both from within and without.
In the adoption of the reverse course he naturally
experienced an effect directly the opposite : he
found, that, each time he gratified the desires of
others voluntarily and at his own expense, he
gave rise to a certain harmonious condition, not
only between himself and others, but likewise
within his inner self.   He had succeeded in silenc-
ing the lower self by means of the higher.   The
voice of approval which he then perceived, was
that of the Universal Spirit itself ; for he had

harmonized his will with that of the Spirit, whose occupation consists in nothing else but the bringing forth of harmony. The more he then followed this mode of action, the more his higher faculties unfolded, at the expense of the lower, until they finally became powerful enough to press these into their service altogether. The same faculties which he has thus encouraged to grow, are now the mediums through which he gathers the higher knowledge and brings himself into conscious communication with the Creator.

Now, however, he makes the same discovery with regard to his gratifications in the sphere of knowledge which he made in respect to those on the material plane : he finds that gathering knowledge is, like any other kind of enjoyment, pleasurable for the time being only. He still has to keep in subjection a personality, and this, being now employed in the acquisition of that which is obtainable in the higher sphere, accordingly accustoms itself also to the higher kind of gratification : it wants more and more ; and thus he would be in danger of once more finding himself alone and in the misery of the world of the self, if the higher, the moral, faculties did not still continue to prevail and accordingly impress upon him the command that the knowledge which they gather

from the Universe is to be used in the interest of
none other than the Universal Spirit; in short,
he feels that the true pleasure of knowledge does
not lie in the personal possession, but comes with
the act of imparting the same to others.   Thus,
from being a benefactor to his fellow-men on the
material plane, he now gradually rises into the
power to benefit them spiritually.   Having himself once been in the condition in which they are
now, and remembering the path which led him
out into a state of greater freedom and serenity,
he proceeds to help them forward in the same
manner as his guides have so far been aiding him.

Now, we are aware that the imparting of knowledge has, in one respect, an effect just the reverse
from that accompanying the bestowal of material
favors: the individual grows richer in that which
he gives.   While he teaches his fellow-men, he
becomes more firmly established in the world of
knowledge himself; for his occupation leads him
into a better understanding of mankind generally,
and therewith also of his own being: His intuitive knowledge, through frequent employment
growing brighter, now shows him the true nature
of their state by reminding him of that of his
own personality in former lives.   He now becomes
convinced of the truth that even the worst of

characters cannot be bad through any other preference than such as arises from an extreme igno-
rance of their true position in the World. Thus
he has risen beyond all tendencies of hating a
fellow-creature. As he continues his occupation
in the interest of the Universal Spirit, it is natural that he should also grow more and more into
the latter's confidence; he acquires a more com-
prehensive understanding of the general plan of
the Universe, because he has proven himself
worthy of taking a more important part in its
affairs. Thus he is led, not alone to perceive, but
also to feel, the great truth that all creatures are
forever bound in one universal brotherhood under
the care of one Father, and that the ultimate destiny of all is a happy one; his faith in the Creator, the self, and the fellow-men becomes firmly
established. Understanding the condition of
those who are still in the dark, his soul now goes
out to them in brotherly sympathy; he does not,
however, love them as they are, any more than he
would love his own former self; he loves them as,
according to his knowledge, they are intended to
become; and this is the feeling which prompts
his greater efforts in their behalf. He sees how
they are destined to wind themselves through the
world of errors and suffering that still lies before

them ; he remembers the many pains which he himself endured, and now he endeavors to shorten the way for his fellow-men by giving them the benefit of his own experience, describing to them what he sees from his higher point of view, and inspiring them with good-cheer and courage. And he perceives that his efforts are not in vain. Wherever the good effect does not immediately come forth, he knows that the spiritual seed which he is sowing is not therefore to be considered lost; he understands the law by which a plant requires for its appearance a certain time. He knows also that, in the realms of the Spirit, all that which does not fall upon good ground must ever return to the sower; for he feels, that, whether his efforts are successful or not, they must invariably cause growth of power within himself. Thus his soul widens out more and more beyond the interests of his personality, making for itself a home in many hearts.

By virtue of this higher activity his power of thought and feeling is raised so far above the self, that, where formerly he was independent of material pleasure only, he now, from the very self-lessness of his nature, becomes indifferent also to personal pain. The subject upon which he has concentrated his whole attention, demands the

sacrifice of all kinds of personal feeling and bodily well-being ; but, at the same time, it gives him
also the power and the gladness of submission ; for
it is a higher form of life, an existence free of
earthly discord, which he now sees lying before
himself and his fellow-men.

A general view of our observations with regard
to the character and life of this man tells us, in
short, that he has guided himself by the truth that
neither pain nor pleasure is contained in the
object in which the soul is centered, but in the
soul itself.   Having perceived that pleasure consists in nothing else than harmony of soul-
vibration, he has naturally made the refinement of
such harmony the one great object of his life ; his
higher faculties have made their growth identical
with this refinement.   From the coarsest, the
physical harmony, he has proceeded to evolve the
finer, the harmony of the soul itself, which becomes manifest in the form of noble character.
This he now radiates into the souls of his fellow-
men as spiritual life-vibration : he gives them of
his higher life.   The vibrations of the soul always
know their source, and so does the soul know them
wherever they may go ; for the soul is independent
of Space.   Thus the pleasure which he gives, the
same does he also feel ; and gradually this higher

harmony so fills his soul that the personal interests dwindle away from his consideration, and at
length become mere means to the one great end :
the evolution of a harmony which is universal.
With this vision before him, he gladly permits his
person to serve as the necessary object for sacrifice.

We observe that in this work in the interest of
the Spirit he not only grows in the power to
receive impressions, but likewise increases his own
vibrative force ; knowledge and power come with
desire and practice.   His manner of life not only
brings forth and develops this mediumship, but
also places the same in his own control.   Having first evolved his selfless character and raised
the same above all material interests, the gift of
prophecy and the various other psychic powers
now unfold within him as naturally, self-evidently,
and beautifully as the flower comes forth on the
plant, unaided by artificial means.   His higher
work has made the possession of the higher powers
a simple necessity, and so these are given him to
wield in accordance with the higher law : his compassion for the suffering body of his neighbor has
procured for his soul the power to heal the same ;
his desire for the welfare of other souls has evolved
within him the power of seeing their path and

guiding them by his will. In using these greater powers solely for the good of his fellow-creatures, he not only remains exempt from the injuries which would result from a selfish use, but his power over soul and substance is bound to constantly increase and eventually to make him the independent master. Formerly, he was dependent upon the Earth-plane, now this becomes subject to his will; and the achievement of this greatness of soul was made possible to him through nothing else than through the evolution of his desire for the preservation of self into the desire for the preservation of *all*. He no more needs a human body. He needs not its pleasures and is not moved by its pains. Nor does the fulfillment of his aspirations require him to maintain a visible personality; for he exerts his powers, not for the sake of showing his greatness and gaining approval, but purely from love of the good work itself.

When, eventually, he has risen out, there is, so far as his personality is concerned, nothing that might attract him ever to return to the Earth-plane in the form of a human being. Having gained the power over the world of earthly substance, his soul now forms, by its own refined vibrative force, a body of such subtility that through it he is enabled to expand over all the

Earth and to penetrate into the souls of men, there to make himself felt, by virtue of his elevating influence, as Divine inspiration. Wherever there are souls which have evolved so far as to be susceptible to this higher influence, there will he be present and make his presence felt. He is not merely an active power, but also a conscious witness of his own influence; his efforts in the interest of harmony have resulted in a higher form of consciousness within himself. He continues, true to his nature, to elevate the souls which are still confined in human form. He helps those who are the nearest to him and who can understand him, so that these, in turn, may use this power for elevating those who are still further in the dark. He breathes harmony and he feels the life of it. His existence is serene beyond human conception. We may form a vague idea of its nature and superiority, when we consider the moments of highest inspiration that come to the soul of man, and when we then bear in mind that the body of this great soul admits of a quality of vibration, or conscious feeling, which is inconceivably finer and greater than that which is attainable through any human brain.

As we have seen, the Spirit creates the Universe with all its living creatures solely for the purpose of demonstrating through these its own being unto itself. Each creature is a living reflector, according to the degree of its evolution, and each is destined to rise forever higher in the conscious understanding of the World. When we consider that the Universe which our minds are to reflect, must ever appear to us as being infinite, and when we also consider how little of its life it is possible for us to know in our present form, and how happy we sometimes feel with that little, — how glorious must be that which is yet to come!

CHAPTER XIX.

OUR RELATION TO THE WORLD OF THE DISEM-
BODIED AND TO ONE ANOTHER.

Now, we are aware that many beings have risen
into this higher sphere and are constantly permeating the souls of men with their elevating influence, helping these to rise into their higher life.
We know also that at certain periods a whole
community sinks back toward a state of spiritual
stupor, once more to become enslaved by the animal
propensities. The higher beings then find it
necessary to demonstrate their presence and their
power to the physical senses. To this end one
of them again takes upon himself the burden of
human life. He descends into the midst of men
as a *Saviour*. As such he proves to them his
power, his authority, over all that is human ; he
demonstrates to their physical eyes and ears the
superiority of the higher law over the will of man,
then he teaches them the first essentials for rising
into this higher power, so that this knowledge
may again become the light of many generations.

He appears to us as *the* Son of the great Father in Heaven. This circumstance draws our attention to the truth that the souls of the higher sphere virtually form *one* soul; and we understand that it is the singleness of their motive which so perfectly unites them. Each finding its happiness solely in the Universal harmony, there is no discordant influence possible from the voices of their self; for there are none such coming forth. Thus it is self-evident that these souls form a perfect harmony also amongst one another, and if one of them takes upon itself an individual existence, it will be only as the representative of all in the accomplishment of their one great object, the evolution of mankind. We may take for granted that not only our Earth is blessed in this manner, but that every heavenly sphere which evolves living beings, likewise evolves such great souls, such Saviours of life, which from time to time descend to the material plane, so that the erring and suffering community may once more be set aright.

While the heavenly beings which dwell in the sphere of our Earth have the power of life to take upon themselves the burden of human sufferings voluntarily, and are impelled to descend to man by their desire of helping him, we find that from the opposite direction there come those which personate the various forms of evil; which must suffer the pains of discord, because they have not yet evolved the power of harmony; and which have not the command over their own motions, but are drawn toward our plane by their personal desire of gratifying themselves. Let us look also into our relation to these:

We have seen that every force in the Universe must constantly alternate between two conditions, its activity being either exterior or interior. While it is in the former state, we perceive its action by means of our physical senses; in the latter condition it is recognizable by those only of the soul, or mind. When a force is thus "invisible," we may know that it is latent. This, of course, applies not alone to the unorganized force, but likewise to the organized, namely, the soul. We have seen that when a soul becomes disembodied, it nevertheless remains intact as a part of the Universal power. It is then latent, awaiting a favorable condition for again coming forth, and, like any other force, it will either reappear as an individual within a physical body, or become more or less distinctly visible alone to the eye of the soul, according to the degree in which other forces coöperate or counteract.

We observe that during its life in a human body there is hardly ever a moment in which some one or more of the soul's faculties are not latent, being at the time hindered from coming forth by the greater activity of the others. We have seen also that during times when animation is suspended, almost the entire soul may disappear from view. Now, when we see the soul become latent at its regular intervals of sleep, we are thereby shown, that, even while the body is strong and healthy, a periodic rest is as indispensable to the constitution of the soul as it is to that of the body; for, the body, being formed and governed entirely by soul-power, can not become inefficient, even temporarily, from any other cause than the counteraction of the soul's activity by surrounding forces. When the soul can be thus deprived of its medium for the third or fourth part of each day, notwithstanding the fact that the power to maintain the usual health and vigor of the body is still efficient, how much longer must be the time of the soul's latency when the body is finally removed from its control altogether! Evidently, that part of the soul which is the direct supporter of the body, needs a far longer period of rest at the close of a life-time than at the end of a day.

Those evil influences which come to radiate their discord into the souls of men, and which are so dangerous because imperceptible to the physical senses, are souls that have once been the possessors of physical bodies, and are, for the time being, bound in a state of latency.   They are human souls which have not yet risen into power over the animal propensities.   The conditions which surrounded their earth-lives have been such that the moral sense of these souls could not properly unfold; and in proportion as the lower self and the intellect have been encouraged, are these souls strong in their desire for self-assertion in the form of discord.   Although such a soul is hindered from forming a body perceptible to the physical senses, it is nevertheless capable of active demonstration wherever it can find favorable soul-conditions.   The only plane on which it can gratify its desires is, of course, the human, because it has itself once been a human ; and from our sphere the call must come : Wherever in a human being the selfish propensities are strong, there the evil soul meets with conditions which allow it to come forth and to assert itself ; for there will be present a soul of like nature; and the same law of affinity by which the happy influence of the higher soul enters the man of noble character, enables also the disembodied evil soul to enter the body of the undeveloped, the selfish man, filling him with its discord and prompting him to give expression to the same in his life.   Thus the evil soul continues to demonstrate itself through the medium of other bodies, to suffer and to cause suffering in this manner, until conditions shall allow it to appear once more in a body of its own for another course of training as an individual man.

Between these two, the Divine soul and the evil, is to be found the multitude of disembodied human souls, each of them bound in a state of latency, until a call arises for its reappearance. There being, of course, as great a variety of disembodied souls as there is of human beings, it is plain that there is not one person who is not continually subjected to the influences coming from this world of the unseen.   According to the nature and the power of his thought will he unconsciously attract to himself the corresponding kind of souls. The same law of thought-transference by which the soul-vibrations may travel from one human-being to another, renders possible also a communication between man and the disembodied soul ; for, in both cases there is the same kind of harmonious vibrations which cannot help but unite in such a manner that each soul must receive those sent out

by the other.   Thus we may know that each of us
is, to a greater or smaller degree, mediumistic.

Disembodied souls may, under favorable conditions, even make themselves apparent to our
physical senses.   However wonderful this may
seem to us, still, we cannot dispute the fact that
such occurrences actually take place, often when
they are least expected.   And why should they
not?   We have abundant evidence, that one person can suddenly appear to another, notwithstanding the space that separates the physical bodies.
This is done by many souls at the moment of their
passing out.   It is evident that in such an event
the dying body itself cannot possibly have any
part.   The soul alone is the actor.   All that is
required for the feat is the power of vibration, the
motive, and the will.   That the soul retains its
power quite independently of the life of its body,
is a truth which we can certainly no longer doubt.
Although counteracting forces hinder the soul for
awhile from appearing to us as a person, it may in
the meantime still exert its vibrative force in other
ways ; for, as we know, the whole World is in
reality nothing else than an infinite variety of
vibrations.   We are therefore perfectly justified
in assuming that many of those mysterious physical phenomena which sometimes force themselves

upon our notice and which are perfectly inexplicable, so far as our present knowledge of Nature's laws can reach, actually have their source in the realms of the disembodied.

We observe also that the faculty of communicating with the disembodied may be developed, so to speak, artificially.   However, when we look more closely into the nature of the process required and into the consequences which may follow, we become aware that this mode of development is as injurious as it is wrong; for the Law is always just.   While observing the mediumistic qualities of the animal, we noticed that these have their source in the circumstance that the animal-mind is not filled with independent thought-forms of a brightness sufficient to obscure that which reflects itself upon the soul direct. The artificial development of mediumship in the human being implies the reëstablishment of this same condition: the mind is to be rendered passive; it is to be freed from thought-forms, so that the invisible may enter and make their impressions felt.   Now, we are aware that man has his power of thought for a well-defined purpose: his intellect is to serve him in the capacity of a "look-out."   It must take note of all that happens within and without; it must see far ahead and all around, study facts and events, cause and effect; it must analyze and combine, and record the results for his immediate use in the work of directing his course through life. The multitude and greatness of the dangers that surround the human being necessitate the constant presence of the power of reason, so that no enemy may come near unperceived and find the man unguarded. This being true with respect to his exterior life, how much more must this truth apply to the life of the soul! We have seen that man's material existence has no other purpose than the evolution of his higher faculties. The intellect, therefore, must ever remain the indispensable servant of these. By its help they are enabled to detect all the evil influences that may come to them from anywhere in the material World or in the World of the invisible, and thus, when necessary, to prevent even a contact with them. Every human being has within him a certain portion of animal propensity, and is therefore in some degree exposed to these influences. In order to rise out of the danger of attracting them, he is compelled to completely eliminate his lower self; and this can be done only through a constant exercise of his intellectual and moral powers. We have seen that this is the kind of exercise through which the higher souls have made themselves worthy of becoming the representatives of the higher thought, and thus we are led to the conclusion that it is also the only medium through which we may attract the wholesome influences.

The character of the ordinary disembodied souls is, like that of any imperfect human, full of error caused by the influence of the lower self. These souls are therefore the ones which are most strongly attracted to that person who has removed from his own lower self the watchful and restraining power of thought. The conditions for the active demonstration of an imperfect soul are in such a case most favorable. The propensities of the person combine with those of the visitor and are thus, in the absence of the reasoning power, in position to play great havoc with all the treasures of the soul that are within their reach ; and they do this. Not only will the feelings pertaining to the self receive encouragement in both parties, but neither one of these will be able to correctly perceive the other ; the visitor will, either consciously or unconsciously, delude the person who attracted him ; for the eye of the self can see only in accordance with its individual nature, and this, we know, is never the same in any two persons, and never faultless in any one.

The truth will thus ever appear distorted; it will every time reflect itself in the mind of the observer in the nature of error. As in every-day life the appearance of persons to each other always conforms itself to the nature of the personal desires prompting each, so may also the disembodied soul which comes to gratify a personal want, conceal itself behind a character which it assumes. The personal preferences may induce the medium, unconsciously to itself, not alone to mistake the identity of its visitor, but likewise to misunderstand the communication received. And in every case we do find this latter tinged with the personal character of the medium, as the reflection of a picture must conform itself to the nature of the reflector. We can easily perceive that such imperfectly understood communications, commands, or informations must always, even if they are of a higher character, cause more or less of mischief to all concerned. On the other hand, it is plain that every communication which results in any kind of personal advantage to either the human beings or the disembodied souls, must, at some time during the process of evolution, be paid for by whomever such advantage has been received by. For, through every material success the human soul gets somewhat of encouragement

in its love for that which is material. Thus each
earthly enjoyment adds its mite to the weight
which hinders man from rising out of the human
plane; and yet, as we have seen, at some future
time he *must* let go. He who is rich, powerful
in worldly matters, and favored with all kinds of
human affection in this life, will surely in some
future one find himself deprived of all; for man
must sometime get a chance to look beyond the
human life, and he cannot do this while his vision
is obstructed by the dense mist of the pleasures
belonging to the ordinary human sphere.

The evil consequences resulting from an artificial development of mediumship are, of course,
most severe upon the medium itself. For, each
time a person offers himself in this manner to promiscuous influences of earth-bound souls, he loses
a part of his control not alone over his body, but
also over his mind. By repeated voluntary absti-
nence from the use of his reasoning powers he
gradually loses his former facility to command
them. We see that the medium of the hypnotizer
unconsciously becomes subject to the desires of
the latter in such degree as to lose its power of
freeing itself from them even in its normal state.
So does this medium of the disembodied souls,
each time it places its powers in their service,

encourage the visitors to monopolize them to a greater extent than they did the last time; and so, eventually, in the absence of the power of intellectual guidance, the whole person becomes the obedient tool of these earth-bound souls, at any time ready to exchange its own identity for theirs. Thus the medium retards the evolution of its own individual character.   It loses more and more also its power of discrimination in respect to the character of its visitors.   Those of the lower order, in accordance with their selfish nature, gradually make themselves the most prominent; and, in consequence, this medium becomes exposed to all kinds of error, great and small, — a soul dependent for its gratifications upon its fellow-beings in the realms of darkness.

All our observations show us that human mediumship is designed to evolve alone through nobility of life.   Selfless thought attracts the selfless soul, and is at the same time the best guard against the influences of the opposite kind.   Until we have evolved a character of great power and goodness, neither are we capable of drawing toward ourselves and consciously communicating with the higher soul, nor are we safe from the harmful influence of the lower.   But, so surely as the artificial development brings forth the hurtful kind of

mediumship, does the natural, through the evolution of a noble character, develop in us the beneficial kind, which must appear in its perfection so
soon as our character proves itself capable of
wielding the higher powers in accordance with the
demand of the higher law, which is *selflessness*.

Meantime, though we may not be clearly conscious of the fact, our communication with the
realm of the disembodied quietly and mysteriously
takes its course, in obedience to the dictates of
the law of affinity, working good and harm on
either side, according to the nature of our thought.
When we contemplate the fact that this mysterious realm, though hidden to the senses of the
ordinary mortal, is nevertheless so near to each of
us that our souls inhale its very atmosphere, —
how awe-inspiring is the nature of this world of
the invisible! and, at the same time, how comforting to us human beings is the knowledge, that
therein are present also the souls of all those with
whom we are bound by the ties of love and friendship! These friendly souls can, if we will, come
even closer to us in their present state than was
possible to them while they were still in physical
bodies of their own. As our friends and loved
ones who are still in this life feel all the vibrations
of kindness that we send out to them, so do also

those who have passed out, and likewise do we receive theirs. In accordance with the nature of this kindness will our influence be either elevating or depressing : while painful longing invariably brings sorrow also to the objects of our affection, our thoughts of selfless kindness inspire them with feelings of good cheer.

Among the multitude of human beings and dis-embodied souls with which a person is connected there certainly is, in every instance, one with whom his nature is more perfectly in harmony than with any of the others : each of us has one particular friend. Now, we see that the strongest kind of human affinity requires that the individuals be of opposite sex : the one must be of masculine nature ; the other, feminine, — the former excelling in power to impress ; the latter, in facility for recep-tion. Let us understand more perfectly the nature of this closest of relationships.

When we look into the principles of harmony from which the Spirit evolves the World, we find that these two elements are already present at the very foundation : we see that they find their orig-inal expression in the relation between Motion and Substance. The masculine, being the force of impressing, is represented by the power of Motion, vibration ; the feminine, in its character of receptivity, is expressed in the vibrating Substance. They are thus originally one, — neither being possible of appearance without the other. The one is the life; the other, that which lives. There can be no surplus of either. Taking a general view of the world of Motion and Substance, we observe that this presents the appearance of a multitude of equally proportioned elements in a state of constant fluctuation from one side of their equilibrium to the other. As we follow them in their course of evolution, we find that the power of motion, as it assumes its higher form, namely, that of organized life, brings forth a more pronounced division also between these two elements, the power of impression and the facility for reception. Already on the vegetable plane, we see these appearing in separate, individual forms, as male and female. In the animal-world this separation becomes still more clearly defined; while, lastly, on the human plane it assumes its most pronounced degree, appearing perfect, not only physically, but likewise with respect to the character of the souls: the masculine nature becomes clearly defined in its preference for independent thought and deed; that of the feminine, in its character of susceptibility, power of feeling. However, as we follow these souls in their further evolution,

as from generation to generation the human society rises in degree of culture, we find that the
masculine soul gradually increases in power of
feeling, while the feminine becomes more and
more independently active and thoughtful. This
slow but sure return of the two elements toward
their original equilibrium is an essential preliminary to their rising into the higher plane of life:
while the power of feeling is required for impelling the soul to expand beyond the self into the
lives of the fellow-creatures, thought is the power
through which this feeling is elevated above the
plane of matter. In the higher sphere the singleness of their selfless motive then enables the
individuals of the two sexes to closely unite with
one another and thus to form one perfect soul,
never again to part. This truth is clearly illustrated to us by the character of the Saviour, who
comes to us as the personification of the highest
form of thought permeated with the purest love.

We have seen that a surplus of any one of
these elements which form the Universe is impossible. We are also aware that the evolution of
each of them must take its course in the form of
a separate individual, whose identity can never be
lost. As these two elements, then, are destined
ultimately to return to their original union; as

they have taken the form of separate souls ; and as, on our plane, each soul, by reason of its difference from every other soul, requires for this perfect union an affinity distinguishable from every other, — we may conclude that the masculine and the feminine elements in the world of man equal one another with respect also to the number of individuals by which each is represented. A surplus of either element, being an impossibility at the very foundation of the World, must also remain such throughout Eternity. Thus we may infer that the various human souls do not exist singly, but in pairs, each of which consists of a masculine and a feminine from one and the same germ. Each such pair forms a like close affinity as every one of the others, and remains thus spiritually related throughout the course of its evolution.

But now the great question arises within us, " Why is the individual so often hindered from forming with the companion of his soul a personal acquaintance ? " For this question, too, we may find an answer : One reason for such repeated separation lies in the fact that in this, as in all other matters, the all-pervading law of contrast rules. We know that this most intimate of companionships implies the highest form of happiness

possible to the human personality.   This feeling,
like all others, can be consciously perceived only
after the soul has personally experienced the very
opposite.   Supposing we all were, from now on,
favored with the blessing of this perfect companionship uninterruptedly from life to life, — how
could we possibly retain within ourselves a clear
conception of the opposite state?   In exact proportion as this would fade from our recollection,
should we become oblivious also to the greatness
of the happiness contained for us in this union
with our dearest friend.

There is another reason why the Spirit from
time to time prevents the personalities of the
counterparts from meeting : it is in the interest
of their evolution into the higher life.   We have
seen that the evolution of the soul implies the
evolution of its desire ; its love must expand
beyond the sphere of the personality.   Now, the
love for our natural companion and for all that
which comes forth from our personal relationship
with the same, belongs altogether to our personal
sphere ; it is natural to our personality, and therefore the exercise of this kind of affection deserves
no special credit ; it is of the nature of a recreation, — a strictly personal enjoyment.   We have
seen, however, that the higher life demands a

higher kind of love, — Divine love, a love that
has for its object the good, not of our own self,
but of our fellow-creatures. While we are tied
with the bonds of personal love, it is not in our
power to rise out and look upon all fellow-men
with equal eye; nor could we then demonstrate such impartiality of feeling by our conduct.
And yet, this is the very power required of the
greater soul. Therefore, so that we may get the
necessary chance for the selfless exercise of our
affections, we are for certain periods removed
from the possibility of bestowing them upon our
friend. We are led to practise self-denial with
respect to human love; and we know that our
power of feeling is not thereby killed, but, on the
contrary, strengthened and elevated; because it
is caused to expand into the great beyond, bringing us ever nearer to the lives of our fellow-beings
and at the same time also to those great souls
who have gone before us. Thus the Spirit
causes during one life-time a separation, so that
the souls may be impelled to work; in another, it
brings them once more together, that they may
enjoy the recreation which their constitutions call
for. Each time they meet, their union is of a
higher nature, until the time arrives when their
affections no more need for their demonstration a

human body; for then the souls will have formed
their final union for life in the great and beautiful
world beyond the self.

When we consider how the two, though originating from the same germ, must leave each other
and then pursue their course of unfoldment,
each in a separate body and in a separate sphere
of action, meeting and parting in alternation;
when we perceive that they are notwithstanding
destined eventually to form their final union as
two souls equally worthy of each other's greatness, — we understand why they must remain in
constant intimate communication even when their
personalities are strangers to each other: the progress of the masculine and the feminine must be
the same in both. Thus each unconsciously
reflects its life upon the soul of the other, and
in return receives a similar impression from its
counterpart. By this means their development is
equalized. And do we not often experience such
peculiar sensations which have not their source in
our sphere? Do not, at certain times, when we
are apparently alone, strange feelings creep into
us that raise us into an unaccountable state of happiness; and, again, do we not as often feel against
our will depressed? Searching for the cause, we
find it not. Such feelings may then be but the

reflections cast upon us out of the life-experiences. which our friend, who may be thousands of miles away, is at that very moment undergoing. Our intuition then prompts us to give the like consideration to these feelings that we bestow upon those arising from our own experiences: the elevating kind we turn into the corresponding actions; the opposite, we make use of as objects upon which to exercise our higher power, — we rise out of them into our wonted state of harmony. Knowing that also our own conditions reflect themselves upon another soul, we find double cause for carefully considering their nature. With each effort that we make, in thought and deed, in the unfoldment of our moral powers, we unconsciously exert an elevating influence upon the partner of our destiny.

Indeed, the more we learn of the nature of our lives, the more clearly do we perceive how impossible it would be for any one of us to work out his salvation independently of his fellow-beings. All our observations of the Universal life convince us that the entire World is but a multitude of close relationships. As not an atom can ever be removed from its intimate connection with its fellows, so *not a soul can ever be alone.* Go where we will, and do what we choose, — we cannot cease

to give and to receive the influences corresponding
to our nature. Though our personality at certain
times seem ever so deserted: as intimately as its
fate is interwoven with those of all its fellow-
creatures, so inseparable is also our soul from its
connection with the world of souls; or the Universe would not continue. The all-powerful, all-
wise, and ever-present Father, who forever maintains intact the close relationship between the
various elements which constitute the world of
matter, will, in His goodness, likewise continue to
provide for this intimate companionship among the
souls which have received from Him their power
to command this World and to employ the same
according to His Law as the medium for their
joint unfoldment. And beautiful indeed will be
their evolution into that higher life, in which they
all are destined to enjoy the like condition of
serene content !

CLOSING REMARKS.

We have, then, at last come to the end of our
journey. It is not possible for us to go still further, — nor is it necessary; for the object of our
wish has been accomplished. When we look back
along the line of our path, and then into the view

that opens out before our eyes from the point
which we have reached, we perceive that kind
Providence has led us through this world of mys-
teries directly into those conceptions of the universal life which were the objects of our search,
and which we find to be so needful to the human
soul as friendly guides through light and darkness.
From having first been made acquainted with the
ideal nature of the World, we have been led to
sense the nature of its Spirit ; we have perceived
the almighty power of harmony which insures the
immortality and the progressiveness of all the
souls of which the Universal life consists. Following their line of evolution, we have then
become aware of their relationship ; we have seen
how on each successive higher plane the harmony
within them and among them grows more complicated and more perfect, thus showing us how all
the souls are forever bound in one close brotherhood in the care of one benevolent and ever-pres-
sent Father. We have observed how Justice
governs our fates and keeps them closely interwoven, so that eventually they all may bring the
like degree of happiness to the respective souls as
these approach their final union in the higher life.
Providence has led us to a point of view ·from
where we may no longer look upon the sufferings

with which we are afflicted, as being utter discords; we know them to be merely dissonances
required by the law of harmony for the right
appreciation of the times of happiness which are
to follow.   Our human pleasures now appear to
us as being but a compromise, allowing our undeveloped soul a temporary rest, an opportunity for
gathering-up its forces; while, on the other hand,
we look upon the hardships as coming to remind
us of the effort necessary for our rising out into
the pleasures of the higher sphere: we see in them
the objects which the soul requires for the evolution of the powers by means of which its noble
destiny may be fulfilled.

Indeed, we have obtained all those conceptions
in which the human heart finds its encouragement
to persevere.   Are they the very Truth?   We
must acknowledge that we shall never be entirely
convinced by our human sense.   There is one
way only in which their nature can become apparent: "By their fruits we shall know them."   It
is a wise decree, that our convictions with regard
to our destiny are not to grow beyond the stage
of our individual unfoldment.   If the human soul,
which is still dominated by the interests pertaining to the self, could look beyond its present life,
foreseeing with its own eye the personal experi-

ences that are to follow in the next, its evolution into higher spheres would be impossible; for all our thoughts and deeds would then invariably be weighted with considerations of a human nature, confining us forever to a life in human form. In order to rise out into that higher sphere in which the souls unite for perfect harmony and happiness, it is necessary that we be free in every way to cultivate the life that harmonizes with the nature of the Universal Spirit: seeking our pleasure in the welfare of all souls alike, loving and encouraging the good *for its own sake only*. It is, then, for this purpose that we are constrained to demonstrate to ourselves the truth of our conceptions by our individual effort : we come into the higher knowledge as we lead the corresponding life. Meanwhile the approving voice which makes itself perceptible within our soul as we proceed in this direction, is to be recognized both as a reward and as a guide : coming to us in the garb of highest pleasurable feeling directly from the Father, who is ever present and within us, it is the generator of our faith. The oftener we succeed in calling forth this voice and the more familiar we become with it, the better shall we understand the nature of its source, — the stronger and more beautiful will be the faith which we evolve; and, again, according to our faith will be the nature of our life.

This faith in the wisdom, the power, and the goodness of our Heavenly Father gives us a never-failing power of glad submission to all the hardships which an inevitable destiny compels each one of us to undergo; no human knowledge can ever so inspire us to gracefully surmount all obstacles that lie in our path. And even to the last, when the end of our present term of life draws near; when, as it may happen, Fortune turns away from us and we are left to end our days in loneliness and trouble, our Father will not then withdraw from our soul the comfort that we shall have earned through our close attention to his voice : then will our faith still gather-in the rays of sunshine coming from the higher World, and in their light we shall find the way through all the cheerless darkness of the moment to see the coming of the brighter time!

The more our life approaches in its nature the lives of those great souls who have gone before us, the stronger will this faith become : at first believing, we shall more and more become convinced; while demonstrating our conceptions, we shall behold their truth, and, together with our knowledge of their truth, will come to us their power, that wonderful power of conviction which so permeates the soul with life and happiness, with love for its Creator and its fellow-beings, that the very force of its expression will raise the soul into the higher sphere.

Our conceptions are to the eye of our soul what the rays of the Sun are to the eye of the body : they reveal to us both the existence and the nature of the source from which they come. All conceptions which generate within our soul a growth of harmony, leading us into a higher life, thereby prove to us that the sphere from which they emanate is the Harmony, the Life itself; and as we direct our course according to their guidance, our Father, who has sent them to us, will surely verify our faith by continuing in the fulfillment of His promise, that, freed from the gloomy world of self, we may truly enter the Kingdom of Heaven.

THE END.

A Bibelot for Book-Lovers.

Price in handsome cloth, $1.25.

Walter Blackburn Harte

MEDITATIONS IN MOTLEY: A Bundle of Papers Imbued with the Sobriety of Midnight.

This is a bundle of papers written in a vein of delightful humor, and filled with those sober and fantastic speculations that appeal to all those lovers of literature who have discovered among the older humorists some of the most agreeable philosophers of their time.

"Meditations in Motley" is a book for the fireside or outdoors; for gray days or sunshine; for solitude or society. It will take its place among those books handy at one's elbow which one instinctively reaches for as one sinks into a cosy armchair in a snug corner and abandons one's self to the seductions of meditation and firelight — and perhaps a pipe of tobacco.

"Motley's the only wear."

The papers are on the most various topics, and throw light on literature and social questions without touching directly the essay in criticism or sociology. "Meditations in Motley" is a book that tumbles out of every category. It is a book of its own kind — as all who know the writer's work can anticipate. The style of the essays reminds the reader occasionally of the older English humorists, but there is added a suggestion of French sparkle and wit and vivacity and lightness of touch.

The History of a Great Social Experiment.

Price in handsome cloth, $2.00.

Dr. John T. Codman

BROOK FARM. Memoirs, Historic and Personal.

A complete history of the famous Brook Farm experiment has been one of those books which demanded writing to complete the most interesting era of American literature and social thought, and at last we have a volume that covers the whole ground adequately — Dr. John Thomas Codman's "Brook Farm: Memoirs, Historic and Personal." Dr. Codman is one of the few surviving members of the Brook Farm community, and his work has, therefore, the special value of intimate personal knowledge of the inner workings of the scheme and of the character and personalities of the group of famous men who were interested in it. The book will have an immediate claim upon the interest of all students of American literature, and of social thought everywhere.

The History of a Great Social and Intellectual Awakening

For sale by all newsdealers, or sent postpaid by
Arena Publishing Co., Boston, Mass.

The Latest Social Vision.

Price, paper, 50 cents; cloth, $1.25.

Byron A. Brooks

EARTH REVISITED.

The New Utopia, " Earth Revisited," is the latest social vision, and in many respects the most charming work of this character which has ever appeared. In it we see the people, the state and the church under true civilization, and the new psychology is introduced in such a manner as to interest students of psychical research.

Here are a few press opinions : —

Richmond, Va. Star

" As a story, it is very interesting."

Chicago Times

" Worthy of consideration for its study of the social and other questions involved."

Review of Reviews

"The story is written in an autobiographical form and pictures the social, industrial, religious and educational America of 1992. As a work of fiction the volume embodies in a fanciful way a view expressed in the closing words: 'To live is to love and to labor. There is no death.' The style is clear and direct."

Lyman Abbott's Paper, The Outlook

"Mr. Brooks is an earnest man. He has written a religio-philosophical novel of life in the coming century. The hero of this story has lived the life of the average man and at length, when he finds himself dying, he wishes that he might have a chance to live his life over. The wish is granted and he is born again on the earth a century later. Social and scientific and religious evolution have in a hundred years contrived to make an almost irrecognizable world of it. Human nature is changed; altruism is fully realized; worship has become service of man; the struggle for wealth and social rank has ended. Mr. Brooks' book is worth reading by all sincere people, and in particular by those interested in Christian socialism and applied Christianity."

Nashville, Tenn. Banner

"If you should happen to pick up Byron A. Brooks' 'Earth Revisited' and read the first chapter, the chances are that you would follow the story on to the end, even if you had other things on hand spoiling for your attention. Summed up, 'Earth Revisited' is a wild though delightful story, short enough to be filled from end to end with throbbing interest and long enough to fully round off the things that are introduced."

www.ingramcontent.com/pod-product-compliance
Lightning Source LLC
Chambersburg PA
CBHW030131030726
47498CB00007B/2656